Readers love the Day and Knight series by DIRK GREYSON

Day and Knight

"This couple works for me, and they both have just enough baggage to make them perfectly flawed characters, which makes me want to cheer all the more for their happily ever after."
—The Novel Approach

"I had a hard time putting this book down… a very captivating book and I hope to see these characters again in the future."
—Hearts on Fire

"I like the premise of the book, liked the characters… we got a nice ending and I see plenty opportunity for a second book."
—Literary Nook

Sun and Shadow

"They have great dialog, are funny and sexy, and I really enjoy watching them together. I'm definitely a fan and look forward to seeing the next phase of their relationship and what the next mission brings."
—The Blogger Girls

"Dayton and Knighton's story is certainly one that needs to be continued."
—Prism Book Alliance

"…I love Day and Knight as a couple. Their bickering makes the whole book that much more fun to read."
—Inked Rainbow Reads

By Dirk Greyson

An Assassin's Holiday

DAY AND KNIGHT
Day and Knight
Sun and Shadow
Dawn and Dusk

YELLOWSTONE WOLVES
Challenge the Darkness
Darkness Threatening

Published by Dreamspinner Press
www.dreamspinnerpress.com

DAWN AND DUSK

DIRK GREYSON

Published by
DREAMSPINNER PRESS

5032 Capital Circle SW, Suite 2, PMB# 279, Tallahassee, FL 32305-7886 USA
www.dreamspinnerpress.com

Dawn and Dusk
© 2016 Dirk Greyson.

Cover Art
© 2016 L.C. Chase.
www.lcchase.com
Cover content is for illustrative purposes only and any person depicted on the cover is a model.

ISBN: 978-1-63477-278-5
Digital ISBN: 978-1-63477-279-2
Library of Congress Control Number: 2016901418
Published May 2016
v. 1.0

Printed in the United States of America
∞
This paper meets the requirements of
ANSI/NISO Z39.48-1992 (Permanence of Paper).

To Becky, for all her continued help.

Chapter 1

"STEPHEN, PLEASE call me back," Dayton Ingram said, leaving his third message. He closed the connection and tossed the phone on his desk. "Son of a bitch," he grumbled under his breath.

"What's got you in a twist?" Knighton asked, coming around the corner and plopping his fine ass, which Day was not supposed to be paying attention to at work, on the side of his desk as though he owned it.

"Stephen isn't returning my phone calls," Day told him with a twist of worry in his gut. "He is always pretty reliable about things like that."

"Maybe he went out into the desert for a few days and can't get a signal," Knight offered logically, but Day wasn't accepting logic at the moment. He was damn worried and getting more so by the hour. "You know your brother can take care of himself. He raised you, so that means he'd be able to survive a head-on train collision, as well as the horsemen of the apocalypse."

"You're fucking funny. Har, har." Day turned away from his asshole partner and tried to concentrate on the screen.

"Okay, so you can't take a joke today," Knight pressed.

"Poke the bear, go ahead," Day growled, turning toward Knight. Hell, if Stephen wasn't here for him to be angry at, then he could take his shit out on Knight.

Knight grinned that off-kilter grin he'd developed just recently for when he seemed to be humoring him, and Day desperately wanted to smack the fucker. The only thing stopping him was that Knight might have actually liked it, and even though their office oozed testosterone out the damn carpet, with all the swagger and former military guys, it would still get him in trouble. Then he'd have to explain what Knight could do to get him that riled up, and he didn't want to answer those questions. Neither of them did.

"Stephen always calls to let me know if he's going to be out of pocket, and even when he was on the road, he called regularly and always returned messages." Day sounded whiny and ground his teeth in frustration. "I'm allowed to be a little worried."

"Maybe he's busy," Knight suggested, this time without the shit attitude. "Don't worry. You said he had a new lady in his life and that he had some business dealings he was trying to finalize, so he's probably really tied up. Have you texted and e-mailed him?"

Day rolled his eyes. "Yes. Both, multiple times. I figure I'd get an 'I'm alive, call you soon' message, but nothing." He balled his fist and wondered if all of this was only residual anxiety from all the activity and action he and Knight had been up to.

In the past few weeks, they had been to Mexico to stop a terror plot, then raced around parts of Europe ahead of rival Russians to recover art lost since World War II in order to prevent a diplomatic coup by said Russians. Now he'd been home three days, and he was still on edge. He didn't walk anywhere; he hurried and raced, even to the bubbler. "Was this how it was in the Corps, after an assignment?"

"The adrenaline, the pace that ran you ragged?"

Day nodded.

"Yeah. Without downtime, you get used to going a mile a minute, and slowing down seems like death." Knight slid off the desk and walked around to where Day sat. "It's something that's hard to get used to. Whenever I wasn't deployed, I used to crawl out of my skin because Cheryl and Zachary took their time to get ready to go places. They always had bags packed, and yet they were never ready when I was. Normal things like that seemed like a complete lack of planning to me. They never moved fast enough and always lagged behind. I had to be the first in line, arrive early, never be late or last—all those things were drilled into me that weren't part of their lives."

"You think that's what this is?" Day's hands went faster, and he noticed he'd started typing like a bat out of hell. Everything he did seemed in a rush, and everyone else moved at a snail's pace.

"We've been home three days, and in the past few weeks, we've each been shot and have been halfway around the world. Yeah, I think you need to get used to the pace of civilian life again. Your brother is most likely out having a good time with his lady, and you're worried because he hasn't called you back."

Knight sounded logical, but Day's stomach didn't agree. Something deep down told him there was something wrong. Not that he could do much about it, and he'd look stupid if he grabbed a flight to Phoenix on a stupid whim. He'd have to wait for Stephen to call back. Stephen would— eventually. "Have you finished your reports?" Day asked, trying to force his mind back on something normal. Maybe something routine would help.

"Yes." Knight lifted his gaze, and Day followed it to the bank of monitors along one wall. The news and other information scrolled across the bottom of their silent screens while political talking heads and newscasters moved their lips. "Looks like Peter came forward with the other pieces of lost art."

Day nodded, watching as four pieces of art stolen by the Nazis, along with the Raphael they had already made public, flashed on the screen. He couldn't make out what was being said, but he smiled at the story. He and Knight had done their jobs, and so had Peter, turning in the stolen WWII art he hadn't known he had, and Day was happy the world had the masterpieces back to enjoy.

"It seems that two of the pieces will go back to their owners or the descendants of their owners, and the others will go back to their museums," Day said.

"You two," Dimato, their boss, snapped in his usual manner as he stopped in the doorway of Day's office. "It's getting late. Go home. You both need to rest, because if you think you're going to coast until after the holidays.... Security threats never take a holiday."

"Yeah, right, when has either of us coasted?" Knight snapped, and Day swallowed hard, wondering what was going on. "We've been going for three weeks and have put healing and our personal lives on hold, willingly." The hard Marine portion of Knight was up and ready to fight. "Sir."

Day turned away because... well, first of all, he didn't want to smile and break the effect. And second, Knight was hot like this: filled with tension, legs apart, firmly planted like it would take a howitzer to move him.

Sometimes Day forgot the power Knight could command.

Day turned back once he'd schooled his expression and wondered what was going on between them. "All right, enough pissing contest," he finally said, trying to defuse the situation. "I can get a ruler." He pulled open his drawer, and both of them turned away at the same time.

"Go home, both of you," Dimato reiterated. "It's late." He turned and walked high and tall back toward his office.

"What's wrong with you?" Day asked as he turned back to his computer to finish up his work. "That's the guy who decides our assignments, and unless you want to get the shit ones for the rest of your life… or fired…." Day shook his head.

"He had no right."

Day sniffed loudly. "Don't get all testosterony. I'm sure he was kidding about coasting, and it was only his way of saying we needed to get out of here while we could." Day saved his report and e-mailed it before locking his computer and getting his bag ready for the weekend.

"What the hell is all that?" Knight asked.

"Work and reading for the weekend. I read the reports of other teams so I can keep up on what's happening. Some are pretty interesting."

"Most are dull as dirt." Knight grunted. "Grab your stuff and let's get out of here."

That was interesting. Knight usually just went home. He didn't hang around and wait for Day on a regular basis. After their first assignment, Knight hadn't spoken to him for the first week, while he'd been recuperating. Day knew Knight had said things would be different when they got home, but he hadn't really thought it would come to pass. Knight had this "what happens on a mission, stays on a mission" thing. Day had hoped it would be different this time, but he hadn't wanted to count on it.

"I need to stop at home," Day said.

"Fine. We can go to dinner from there." Knight turned and strode in his stiff, military way back toward his desk.

Day momentarily forgot what he was doing as he watched Knight's ass in perfectly pressed dress pants. He blinked and turned back to what he was doing in case anyone saw. He finished packing up, grabbed his bag, and left the office, then went right to his car and drove home. He figured Knight would be right along after him, and he had a few things he needed to do before he was ready to go.

He parked in his spot and walked up to his apartment, getting the mail out of the box on the way. He climbed the stairs and let himself in, dropped the mail on the table, and then hurried to the bedroom. The shirt he'd been wearing had been itching him all day, so he took it off, grabbed a comfortable, deep blue, long-sleeve pullover, and slipped into it. He sighed at the softness. When the door buzzer rang, he let Knight in.

"You could have waited."

"You didn't," Day said. "I wanted to change, and I knew you'd be impatient."

Knight grunted.

"Do you want something to drink or to go straight to dinner?" This dating-type thing was different. They'd eaten together plenty, and Day had spent an awkward, snowy night at Knight's house once. There was no pattern to go by. On a mission they generally got along and knew their jobs and their roles. The excitement and energy also seemed to bridge the physical gap between them—most of the time spectacularly.

"What do you have?"

Day went to the refrigerator and got a couple of sodas. He brought them over and handed one to Knight. He wasn't sure if he saw gratitude or annoyance in Knight's eyes. He could be so hard to read. "I have beer if you really want one." Knight was still fighting some demons, one of them being the bottle he'd told Day he crawled into after the death of his wife and son. Day wanted to be supportive, even if a beer would have felt good right then.

He motioned to the sofa, and Knight took a seat. They opened their cans and sipped. Day wasn't sure what to talk about, and Knight stared at the walls, silent and seemingly content to stay that way. It drove Day crazy. "Is there something interesting about my wall?"

"No. Just thinking. Has your brother called or anything?" Knight asked.

"Nothing." The worry that had abated came roaring back, and Day pulled out his phone and sent an *Are you alive?* text, hoping for some sort of response.

"You said he was buying a house?"

"Stephen is going to settle down. He's apparently flipping one house and hopes to make a lot of money, so he got a place in Phoenix."

"Do you have an address?" Knight asked.

Day nodded. "Of course."

"If you don't hear anything, I have some Marine buddies who live out there. I can ask one of them to drive by the house to see if anyone is there." Knight's network of guys he'd served with never failed to surprise Day.

"Thanks. I'm hoping you're right and this is just me overreacting."

Knight paled and drank his can empty like it was a shot to brace himself. "I remember that feeling. I kept trying to call Cheryl, and all I got was voice mail. Texts weren't returned, and e-mails went unanswered. I told myself that it was nothing... until I got the call from the police."

Knight's voice held a softness that Day only heard when he talked about the family he'd lost. Granted, it wasn't very often. Sometimes Day hated it, because there were times he wished Knight thought of him in that kind, gentle way. Mostly it reminded Day that Knight did indeed have a heart under his hard exterior and behind his stubborn assholeness.

"Thanks so much. You really know how to reassure a guy." Day called again and waited for four rings before getting voice mail. He hung up without leaving yet another message. "If I don't hear something soon, I'll take you up on your offer."

"I didn't mean to upset you." Knight set his can on the table beside the leather sofa. "I was taking another trip down memory lane. Nightmare road. Whatever you want to call it. Your brother is fine, and you have nothing to worry about." Knight clapped him on the shoulder. "Didn't mean to be maudlin."

"Does it happen often?"

"Me getting maudlin?" Knight asked. "You should know that. You've seen me like this more than anyone else, except Mark."

Day smiled. "I was going to say acting human."

"Smartass," Knight quipped. "Let's go to dinner."

Day nodded and took the cans back to his tiny kitchen, rinsed them, and put them in the recycling. Then he got his coat from the back of the chair and carried it with him to the living room.

"Day," Knight said, turning around from the table beside the door. "The mail must have scattered when I closed the door." He held an envelope in his hand. "This has no return address and a Phoenix postmark. It was mailed four days ago." He walked over and placed the letter in Day's hand.

Day looked down at it. "Stephen never sends letters. He calls. This must be junk mail. They try to make it look important," he said even as he broke the seal on the envelope. He pulled out the single piece of paper and opened it.

> *I'm in some trouble. I may be out of communication for a while, but I'll call you as soon as I can. Don't worry. I know what I'm doing, and I'll be in touch as quickly as I'm able.*

The note was unsigned, but Day would recognize his brother's scrawling handwriting anywhere.

He handed the page to Knight and turned away, heart pounding, wondering what in the hell he was going to do. "Don't worry?" he asked out loud. "Don't worry! What the hell is going on? My brother has spent years roving the country and living the life of the free with no commitments." Day sat. He had the answer to one question, but a million more raced through his head, all of them ugly and churning his insides.

"You don't know what he means," Knight said, peering over his shoulder.

"He sent me a note, unsigned, instead of calling to say he was in some kind of trouble. If it were 'Hey I'm a few bucks short,' he'd call. This is serious."

"How can you be sure?"

"I know my brother. He always calls back, and he answers e-mails and texts, which he hasn't in days. Now I get this strange note, and you ask me why I think he's in trouble?" Day huffed and began pacing the tiny space in his living room. "I need to get out there and see what's going on."

"But you don't know anything. He may have taken care of whatever this trouble was and will call you tonight or tomorrow."

Knight's making light of this was getting under Day's skin so badly he was back to wanting to hit him.

"Take a breath and think for a minute. When you talked to him last, he didn't mention anything out of the ordinary?"

"No…. Well, that he had a great real estate deal that was going to make him a good deal of money. That's definitely unusual. Maybe something went sour there." Day continued tracing the perimeter of his living room and tried to think, but his head was muddled with worry, and he fucking hated it. He and Knight had been shot at more than once and he hadn't been this afraid. He'd found out he was cool under fire, but this….

Knight left the room, heading toward the kitchen, and Day let him go and continued pacing. He wanted to call and leave another message, this time screaming at Stephen for being a complete and total asshole. When Knight returned a while later, carrying two plates, Day hadn't registered how long he'd been gone.

He slipped a plate into Day's hand. "Eat. You need to take a minute and think. Don't get wrapped up in your emotions. That clouds your judgment and encourages rash decisions. When was the last time you saw your brother? Was it last Christmas?"

"Yeah. He came here for a week and then flew out west again."

"And he seemed normal then?" Knight took a bite of his sandwich but didn't seem to taste it. His attention was focused like a laser on Day. Under different circumstances, Day would have been flattered, even aroused, by the intensity.

"Yes. Just like he always was." Day's hand shook when he picked up the sandwich, and he stilled it consciously, taking a bite but tasting sawdust. He ate anyway, trying to think of anything from any conversation he'd had with his brother that would lead him to believe Stephen was mixed up in something. He came up with nothing. Stephen was so carefree and had so much joy for life, especially these last few years. "I can't think of anything." Day handed Knight his phone. "You can bring up the texts. There's nothing there. His e-mails are the same, just talking about general life stuff. No hint of trouble."

"Okay. Is Stephen levelheaded?"

"Yeah," Day answered. "That's part of what worries me. He doesn't go off half-cocked, and he doesn't push the panic button. He stepped in to raise me when I needed his help. Stephen is calm and kind of mellow.

Things that bother other people roll off his back. So a message like this would never be sent unless something bad had happened." Day finished his sandwich. "I have to go find out what I can."

"What?" Knight asked, setting down his plate. "No way. You need to think about this. You could be going on a wild goose chase. You don't know anything about what's going on or how bad it really is."

"Doesn't matter," Day said. "I have to go. What if he's in real trouble and needs my help?"

"I just warned you about emotional decisions." Knight glared at him. "You're always the one who looks into everything before assignments. You researched mines, and paintings, found locations, and hunted down people before our last assignment. But here you want to rush in blind."

"I don't have much choice. My brother could be hurt or worse…." The thought was like a fist around his heart. "He's the only family I have. What would you do if Cheryl had sent a note like that?" Day knew he wasn't playing fair, but what the hell. "You'd have been there in two seconds, guns blazing, and don't tell me anything differently. You know you would." He held Knight's gaze until he nodded once. "So what should I do?"

"First thing, we go into the office tomorrow and start looking into what's going on out there. See if there's a trail you can follow. Do the groundwork before you run off. Who knows, by this time tomorrow, you may have heard from him and everything will be fine. And if not, you'll know something more than you do now." The expression in Knight's eyes told Day what he expected to find. Knight was blowing smoke up his ass to try to get him to calm down and think. While he appreciated the sentiment, he hated the prevarication.

"All right," Day agreed. "We'll look and see what we can find." He stood, grabbed his bag, pulled out his computer and hooked it up, then logged remotely into the system using encryption and his passkey. "If we're going to research, we might as well start now. It isn't like I'm going to be able to get any sleep." He turned to Knight and was met with resistance.

Then Knight's shoulders slumped slightly and he rolled his eyes. "Aw hell." Knight pulled out a chair and sat next to him.

"You can go if you'd like," Day said.

"Fuck no. If I do, you'll probably find something and be on the next plane to Phoenix. I need to make sure you keep your head on straight."

Day wasn't sure if he should be insulted or not, and after tensing, getting ready to take Knight's head off, he recognized Knight might be worried about him and this was his clumsy way of expressing it. "Fine."

He got logged in and searched his brother's name, which showed him information he already knew.

"Try federal databases," Knight suggested, and Day turned to him. "It's worth a shot."

"Why suggest that? Not that I won't try, but it seems an odd suggestion."

"It's as good a place to start as any, and a lot of agencies keep a lot of information. As former NSA, you understand that. So see if there's anything unusual."

"I wish you had your computer. Then we could double-team this," Day said and set up some searches, getting them running. Of course, they came up with nothing he didn't already know.

"Try Arizona DMV," Knight said.

"I will," he retorted testily. "Just give me five minutes." He was already frazzled, and Knight looking over his shoulder, backseat typing, was more than a little annoying.

"Is that the address you have?" Knight asked when he got his vehicle information, and Day nodded. "Search it on Google Earth. Let's see what it looks like."

"Is that really going to help? Or are you getting off track? Fine. He said he was looking to settle down, so he may be using that location for his mail. At one time he was living out of his motorhome, but it's hard to keep track. I've been busy, and it seems he has as well." Day got a look at the address and was surprised to see a nice, small house, beautifully kept, with an arid garden in the front and what looked like a touch of green, probably artificial grass, for the yard. Day was realizing there was quite a bit about his brother he didn't know.

"Who owns the house?" Knight asked, and Day figured it was best to let him do the driving. Knight was thinking more clearly than he was.

"It appears to be owned by a Clark Miller," Day said.

"Go back to the DMV database and see what else you can find at that address." Knight stepped away as Day complied, pulled up the information, and then stopped dead in his tracks. "What is it?"

"Look," Day said, pointing. "That's my brother. It's a different picture, and his hair is shorter, and Clark has glasses." Day brought up both images and placed them side by side. "You'd think they were relatives rather than the same person, but it's definitely him."

"My God, why would your brother have two different identities?"

Dayton wished to hell he had the answer to that question.

Chapter 2

KNIGHT WOKE on the sofa in Day's apartment. His neck and back ached. Day still sat at the table, computer in front of him, but as Knight watched, he became convinced Day was asleep sitting up. His fingers rested on the keyboard without moving. Knight groaned as he got to his feet, checking his watch. It was after two in the morning. He quietly went to Day and helped him to his feet. The computer screen woke up and went to a log-in screen, so Knight figured it was fine for now.

"You need to go to bed."

"I need to figure out what happened to my brother," Day said with little fight.

"The problem will still be there in the morning, but right now you're exhausted and not in any condition to help anyone." Knight turned out the lights and made sure the door was locked, then guided Day down the tiny hallway to the bedroom. "Get undressed and into bed."

"But what am I going to do?"

"Go to sleep. Things will be clearer in the morning." Knight laid Day down on the bed and got him out of his shoes. He wondered if he should undress him, but Day got to it, and when he was down to his underwear, he climbed into bed.

Knight turned out the light before leaving the room. He made sure everything was off and rechecked the locks out of nervous habit before returning to Day's room. It was so late, and he wasn't in the mood to drive. He hoped Day wouldn't mind. He got undressed and carefully climbed into the bed, making sure to leave room between them. This whole relationship… thing… whatever the hell it was… with Day had him more confused and turned around than a weathervane in a tornado. He got comfortable and was about to roll over when Day rolled onto his side and slid an arm around Knight's waist, holding him tight.

Day snuffled and made a few sleepy sounds, coming closer until he was tightly pressed against him. "Is nice," Day murmured and stayed asleep.

Knight blew air out his mouth and did his best to go to sleep. This wasn't the first time they'd slept together, but his body and mind had definite other ideas. His head filled with pictures of Day's golden skin and lean muscle, prowling over him. This was not the time for romantic images or to let his damned imagination get the better of him.

Not that it mattered. Knight forced the images and wishes away. This was the worst time. Day was worried about his brother and needed some comfort and care. That didn't make this any more than that. Not that he was going to stand by and let anyone hurt Day—or his family, for that matter. Shit, all that left his head spinning, and he was grateful when sleep claimed him.

"ARE YOU really determined to do this?" Knight asked when Day got out of bed and informed him that he needed to book a flight. "You need to see what's going on before you just jump in." He was still half asleep, and Day was already tearing through the apartment, pulling clothes out of the closet and a suitcase from under the bed.

"I need to find out what's going on with my brother, and staying here—running Internet searches and combing databases—isn't going to get me any closer. I need to be there where he is and try to track him down." He threw open the suitcase and began tossing in clothes, making one heck of a mess.

"What is this? Packing for a Barbie weekend?" That stopped Day in his tracks. "My sisters used to pack like you are for their sleepovers. Okay, first thing, call Dimato and explain what's happening. He has more contacts than either of us. I'll ask one of my friends to go by the house and take a look. Just relax. Pack a bag if you feel you have to, but give yourself a chance to breathe." Knight stepped out from under the covers and immediately shivered. It was cold in the room, and he was wearing only his boxers. He put that from his Marine-trained mind. "You aren't being productive." He gently took Day's hands. "This is a time for thinking and planning, not rushing and running. You aren't accomplishing anything other than riling yourself up."

"You think Dimato can help?"

"You work for him. It's his job to help." Knight tugged Day back toward the bed and put the suitcase on the floor. "It's 6:00 a.m. on a Saturday, and you've only had a few hours of sleep. You can't call anyone right now, and if you want my honest opinion, you're punchy." Knight pulled Day onto the bed and got him under the covers.

Knight waited for the warmth to surround them and for Day to fall back to sleep, though Knight knew he wasn't likely to himself. He'd gotten up early. Too many years to break that habit now. So an hour later, with Day still asleep, he got up and began making phone calls. Knight was just finishing when Day wandered in, wrapped in a robe—lured, no doubt, by the scent of coffee.

"How long have you been up?"

"I called Dimato, and he said he'd see what he could find out about your brother. I gave him both names. He was going to get people digging. He said if you wanted to go, you could take vacation time."

Day nodded.

"I called Holsten, a Marine friend. He never sleeps much, and he's going to go by the house this morning. Don't know how much he'll be able to tell us, but he said he'd take a look."

"You've been busy," Day said with a worried yawn. Knight could feel as soon as Day's nerves got going, like a thunderstorm on the horizon that got closer and closer until the air crackled with energy. "I—"

"Give things a little time. When we find out something, anything, you can decide what you want to do." He still wondered if Day wasn't blowing all this completely out of proportion. The only thing he kept coming back to was the different identities. They had gotten lucky in finding them, and Knight had a suspicion that Day's brother wasn't entirely what Day thought he was. Either he'd gotten himself on the wrong side of the law and had been able to build a fake identity, or he was on the right side of the law… and that opened yet another series of possibilities, none of which was likely known to the man standing in his robe in the kitchen, about ready to jump out of his skin.

"I found very little out about this Clark Miller, other than some basic information. He has a different DOB than Stephen and went to different schools."

"Then you found out quite a bit," Knight corrected. "Whoever created this identity laid a decent back trail and history so it wouldn't look fake. Does the Clark Miller identity have a police record or prison record?"

"Why?" Day asked.

"If it does, then law enforcement or some sort of official channels were involved in creating it. A fake ID built by a criminal would want to make Clark look better than the real person, not worse."

"Wait." Day stalked over. "You think Stephen is a criminal? That he did something wrong? He's my brother. He raised me and helped teach me to be who I am. He taught me right from wrong and had a strong sense of justice and fair play. He's not a criminal."

Knight sat calmly and let Day get it out of his system. "Just check," he said. "Emotion isn't going to help us. Thinking clearly will. This identity was created by someone, because your brother can't be both Stephen and Clark at the same time. We know that Clark doesn't really exist, so get all you can on Clark. We can assume that some of it is close to the truth, while important parts are made to deceive. That's how these are created, for a purpose. We need to divine the purpose behind this one. And it will give you something to do instead of splitting apart." Knight drank his coffee. "Go get dressed, and we'll go to into the office while we wait and see. They might know more. And try your brother again too."

"Bastard," Day grumbled half under his breath and stalked out of the kitchen.

Knight stayed put and didn't jump when the bedroom door closed more loudly than was necessary. He rinsed his mug and left it in the sink.

Day came out of his bedroom, went right to his computer, and logged in.

"Your shirt is inside out," Knight said, and Day growled again, pulling it off. The room was cool, but Knight put his hands on Day's bare shoulders, stroking and kneading the muscle while he worked.

This was not a time for amorous activity, but even though Knight's libido didn't kick in fully, it remained on simmer, like it had for much of the night. Day didn't need to be overpowered or taken to bed, but Knight thought he could use some closeness, some touch and tenderness to ensure he understood he wasn't completely alone.

THE FUNERAL was over, and Knight had come back to their house—now just his house—for the first time since the death of his wife and child. Cheryl and Zachary were everywhere—in pictures, even the remote control truck Knight nearly tripped over as he closed the door. He'd stayed away on purpose. Mark and his wife had put him up because the thought of setting foot in here was more than he could bear. Not that either of them had said a word; they just knew and opened their home.

Knight inhaled and caught the scent of red sauce, the remnants of the last meal Cheryl had cooked, hanging in the air. The first open window would blow that part of her away. Everything Knight did seemed to take him farther from his wife and son. He picked up the offending truck and held it. He had never considered himself sentimental about anything, but now he needed to hold on to what was left of them. He climbed the stairs and went to Zachary's room first, putting the toy in its place on the shelves, the scent of his son surrounding him until it, too, faded away.

Their room was next, and Knight stared at the bed with the fussy comforter Cheryl had insisted on. Knight had never liked it, but now he pulled it off the bed and wrapped it around him, closing his eyes and trying like hell to feel something of Cheryl.

Empty. The house was empty. The bed was empty. So was the room. The silence mocked him, and all he could think was that this was how it was going to be: a life of silence and emptiness. Knight dropped the comforter back onto the mattress in a heap and slowly shuffled down the stairs, only half seeing where he was going. Through the hall and living room, stubbing his toe on the leg of the sofa, hissing at the pain while at the same time reveling in it—something physical to match the ache inside.

He continued to the dining room, opened the built-in cabinets, and pulled out a bottle of vodka. This would do. He needed it. Anything to dull the ache and fill the emptiness. He unscrewed the cap. It fell from his hand, dinging on the wood floor. He didn't care. He wasn't going to need it again.

"KNIGHT," DAY said softly, and when Knight blinked, he saw Day looking up at him. His hands rested on Day's shoulders, unmoving, forgotten.

"Sorry." He pulled his hands away. Loneliness was something he knew very well. It had been his one companion for the past two years. Only the last few weeks with Day had begun to change that, and now things were pulling Day away from him. Knight wasn't sure how he felt about any of this. He had no clue what he was to Day, or for that matter, what Day was to him. He knew they had been together a lot since they had been given their first joint mission. But if Day went off and got himself in trouble he couldn't extricate himself from because of his brother….

Knight stepped away and slowly paced the living room, wanting to look over Day's shoulder but knowing he'd only annoy him. There were definite times to annoy Day. He liked getting a rise out of him. Nothing brought a smile to his face faster than Day's exasperation at something Knight had done, especially when he did it for just that purpose. But this was not the time to push. Day was already too keyed up and getting worse by the minute.

"Put your shirt on or you'll get cold." Knight handed the garment to Day, and Day shrugged it on as he glanced at the screen. "Find anything?"

"Maybe. It's hard to tell since I don't have a Social Security number for this fake person yet. I'm trying to find one. If someone went through the trouble to create an identity like this, they wouldn't miss something that obvious." Day went back to work, digging electronically until he had what he wanted. Then he checked on criminal history.

Knight watched and waited. "Is there a prison record? If there is, I suspect it's for something like armed robbery or maybe a drug offense. Violent but not sensational."

"Yes. Possession with intent to deliver, six months, and one for armed robbery, a year. Both served in Massachusetts." Day turned to look at him. "How did you know?"

"Whoever was making up the history needed it to be serious, but not bad enough to hit the papers and media. It also had to be far away from where he was working. Gives him street cred without being too traceable. Multiple stints means he's a repeat offender, so he's also likely to be willing to get involved in other enterprises. If I were a betting man, I'd say that Clark Miller is an identity made up by a law enforcement agency of some type. That gives us a place to start."

"But it doesn't get us any closer to Stephen."

"Please. Where is the logical Day who was with me a week ago? We know more, and if we learn who set up the identity for him, then we can find out who he's working with and where to put pressure to find out what he was doing."

"That's just it. I can't find out anything." Day sighed and got up, stretching. "There is no record of this Clark Miller working with anyone in law enforcement. Of course, there wouldn't be, because he's made up, and it isn't like they would have Stephen on the payroll openly. It would all be secret and hidden behind security clearances I don't have."

"Never stopped you before," Knight said with a grin.

"I don't know where to look. Could be local, state, or God knows how many federal agencies." Day snatched up his phone and called once again.

Knight's phone rang. It was Dimato.

"Can't find anything," Dimato said. Not that Knight was surprised. "On either identity. I suppose Day already dug up what I was going to tell you about Miller's record."

"Yes," Knight answered levelly.

"There has been an incident at the address in question. No details are being released, and the local police are being tight-lipped, at least for now."

"No idea at all?"

"No."

"I asked a friend to drive by and take a look." Knight watched Day. "Don't know what he'll find, but it's a set of eyes."

"What do you think?" Dimato asked, and Knight turned away and wandered toward the front of the building.

"I think Ingram is going to go no matter what. It's his only family, and if he stays, he isn't going to be worth a thing. What do you think of the alias?" Knight asked, hoping for a confirmation of his opinion.

"Law enforcement setup," Dimato answered. "Bad, but not too bad. Seems like a deep cover of some type. Don't really know, though, and no one is talking, if they know anything." He sighed, and Knight heard swearing under his breath. That could be good or indicate a shitstorm. "Go with him and find out what the hell is going on. Keep expenses to a minimum, find this wayward brother if you can, and then get him back here. We need both of you hale, whole, and ready for action."

"You want me to go?"

"Yes. I don't send agents out alone, and this situation just became of agency interest if it's going to put him out of commission and, by extension, you as well."

Knight wasn't sure why Dimato was being so gracious at the moment. The agency wasn't huge on doing things that weren't billable to someone, and this definitely wasn't. "You're sure?" Knight questioned.

"You want your partner to go into this alone?" Dimato snapped. "He doesn't know what he's walking into, and you'd send him out there to face it by himself."

Knight bristled at the mocking tone. "Of course not," he bit right back. "I was merely wondering why you were prying open the purse strings." He kept his tone light. He wasn't sure what it was about Dimato that had been rubbing him the wrong way lately, but he needed to get it under control. He wished he knew what about his boss raised his hackles.

"You really are a colossal pain in the ass," Dimato said without much heat, but he didn't offer an explanation or answer Knight's question. "Make travel reservations and get out there, figure out what the hell is going on, and then get home before I decide to hang up and fire both your asses." Dimato disconnected, and Knight shoved his phone back in his pocket.

"Who was that?" Day demanded testily from behind him.

"Dimato. He said we should go investigate what's going on with your brother. Pack a bag and get ready to go. I'll get us on the next available flight."

"You're going too?" Day asked.

"Of course I am," Knight bellowed much more loudly than he intended. First Dimato and now Day questioning his enthusiasm for backing his partner was really pissing off his Marine pride. "Did you find anything else?" he asked harshly, switching the topic of conversation.

"No," Day said and went to his room, closing the door with enthusiastic frustration.

Knight understood how Day felt but left him alone, his own frustrations coming to the fore. But there was nothing he could do about them. He'd been preaching about thinking and rationality to Day, so he couldn't let his anger get the better of him.

He made some phone calls and was able to get them on a flight that afternoon. They were going to be subject to intense security screening because of the rapidity of their trip, which meant his tricks for air travel weren't going to work, but that was fine. He could get weapons and anything else he needed from his buddies in Phoenix. It was good to have the kind of friends only Marine brotherhood could provide.

As he was finishing the arrangements, he got another call. "Holsten," Knight said with happy caution. He was thrilled to talk to his friend but afraid of what he had to tell him.

"I drove by to look at the house, and there were police in front and crime scene tape everywhere. They weren't saying anything, but the neighbors were talkative enough. It seems that someone was killed in the house: a woman, apparently the girlfriend of the guy who lived there. They said he hadn't been home in a few days, and the resounding neighborhood opinion, if it means anything, was that he wasn't home when it happened."

Holsten always did have the gift of gab and could get anyone to talk about anything. Now that Knight looked back at things, if he'd have been closer to his friends, he might not have had as tough a time with his grief. He'd closed himself off in his despair, and that might have been the exact wrong thing to do. But fuck if he knew.

"There was an ATF team there, so drugs could have been involved. I don't know much, just what I got from looking. If I had to guess, they'd been there for hours. Did you know the guy?"

"Not personally. My… business partner here is his brother, and he's been worried sick."

"You on your way out?" Holsten asked.

"Yeah."

"Stop by. I'll give you the lowdown if anything else happens. Clarise's sister is a police officer, so she might be able to help. Can't promise anything, though. They can be tight-lipped as hell."

"Just like us," Knight teased, and Holsten grunted.

"I'll see if I can find out who it was in the house. Call when you get out here." He disconnected, and Knight went looking for Day.

He found Day sitting on the edge of his bed, staring at the walls. It seemed he'd hit a mental wall of some sort. "Was that your friend?"

"Dang, you have good ears. Yes. Holsten said that your brother's house is a crime scene. A woman, according to the neighbors."

Day shivered. "Stephen said a little while ago that he had a girlfriend. Things were new between them, but he was excited and seemed happier the last time we talked." He paused and sighed. "This is a nightmare."

Knight sat next to him. "I have plane tickets for this afternoon. But you have a choice to make before we do anything. The police are there, and they're going to pick up your brother's trail, whether he's involved or not. I'm not saying he is, so don't bite my head off," he added preemptively. "The police are going to want to find him."

"What choice?" Day finally asked after sitting still for a full minute at least. "There is no choice. I need to go out there and find out what the hell is going on. He's my only family, and I sure as hell am not going to let the police in the land of moronic sheriffs who put prisoners in tents in the desert get their hands on my brother. I'm going to go out there, find him, and figure out what in the hell all this is about." The fire in Day's eyes was a welcome sight.

"Then get your ass moving and don't spend all day staring at the wall. My car is going to be leaving in half an hour, and you need to have your shit packed, ready, and in the damn car by then. So move your tight ass." Knight stood and stared at Day, who got to his feet and finished packing. He still looked a little like the walking dead, but at least there was some sort of energy other than fear coming from inside him.

"Knight, I'm scared," Day admitted ten minutes later, as he closed his suitcase.

"Of course you are, but what have I told you about fear?"

"Either you use it to make you sharper, or let it debilitate you and make you completely ineffective," Day said.

"That's fucking right, and how are you going to deal with this fear?" Knight pressed.

Day's eyes cleared in seconds, and his posture straightened. He strode out to the dining area, and Knight heard him packing up his computers while Knight got the bags to begin loading the car. Day met him on the way back in.

"That's the last of it. Let's go!" He was already marching toward the car.

Chapter 3

EVEN IN December, Phoenix was warm. Day stepped outside the airport terminal, doing his best to keep the tension and worry at bay. Knight was right; he knew it. Hold the fear inside and let it keep him strong and give him an edge.

"Where are we going?" Day asked.

A huge midnight-blue truck pulled up, and a large man—bigger than Knight—got out and ran around the side, then pulled Knight into a hug and lifted him off the ground while he cackled like an idiot. "It's been way too fucking long, man. Too long." He set Knight back on his feet and became serious. "I was sorry to hear about your wife and son. It burned us all up."

"Thanks," Knight said with more overt emotion than he usually showed to anyone, except maybe in those few unguarded moments they'd had together. Knight turned to him. "This is my partner, Dayton Ingram. Goes by Day, and don't let the curls and sunny disposition fool you—he's got the guts of a brother. Day, this is Colt Holsten."

"No shit?" Holsten said, extending his hand and taking Day's in an iron grip that Day returned measure for measure. "Cool." Holsten let go and began hoisting their bags into the back of the truck. "Let's get going. We can jaw on the way." He looked around as though he expected to be overheard, and then they got in.

"Holsten always thinks someone is listening," Knight murmured just loudly enough for Day to hear. "Good man, can be scary."

"I got that," Day said and crammed himself into the backseat of the cab. He sat with his legs to the side to keep them from under his chin.

Colt slammed the door. "I went by that house one more time, and there's tape everywhere. The cops must have gotten most of what they want because there's only tape left. The story has hit the news. There was one dead woman, no name released yet." Colt pulled out and kept talking. "But I'm betting you know who it is."

"My brother had a new girlfriend, and I think it's her. I never met her, and he didn't tell me anything because he didn't want to jinx it."

"I doubt that's the whole story, then. If he just met her, why was she there? The neighbors said the owner has been gone for days. Unless she was sneaking around and stopped by to get something. But no guy is going to give a new girlfriend a key." They reached the freeway, and Colt kicked the truck into high speed.

"Thank you for looking for us. Day was worried when he couldn't contact his brother," Knight said.

"There's more to this than a brother going off the grid. Him gone, a dead body...." Colt turned to Knight and then glanced back at Day before returning to his driving. "You can't shit me."

"No. But there are things we can't tell you either. It's going to sound like bullshit, but the less you know, the safer you are," Knight said. "What we know is confusing as hell. Whatever Day's brother got involved in is probably bad enough or big enough to kill for. You and your family don't need that ending up on your doorstep."

Colt humphed. "Just let them try." He continued driving like a bat out of hell. "I have what I need to protect myself and my family." He turned to Knight. "Did you leave me hanging when we got in the thick of it in Panama? That was a shit show, but you got me out."

Those words sent a chill up Day's spine. He knew Knight's wife and son had been killed because of something that happened in Panama. Knight had so far refused to talk about it at all, instead backing away from his desire to find out what happened in favor of what Day guessed was a measure of peace in his life. Day couldn't help wondering just what this pivotal event in Panama had cost Knight and the other men who'd gone with him on that mission.

"We were brothers, are brothers. That's what we do—watch each other's back and get each other out of shit. But this isn't like that. This isn't brotherhood, but God knows what being brought to your doorstep." Knight's breathing hitched and quivered. "I paid a huge price for what happened then, and I don't want you to pay the same way. Not now, not ever."

Colt turned and stared at Knight for a second. "You mean what happened had something to do with that?"

Knight nodded.

"That's hell, man. We did what we had to do, you know that. There was no choice for you or any of us. We had orders and we followed them." Colt banged his hand on the steering wheel hard. "Fuck."

"Yeah."

Day sat quietly, hoping Knight would let something slip that would give him a place to start looking into what the mission had been. All he'd done was run into walls of security and classified designations half a mile high.

"I'm sorry, man. I didn't know," Colt said.

Knight lapsed into silence, and Day sat back, offering nothing, soaking in what information he could get.

"That ain't right," Colt muttered after a while.

Day found himself nodding, and Knight muttered his agreement. Not that there was anything they could do about it at the moment. Maybe at some point, Day could get Colt alone and find out what had happened, though he wasn't hopeful. He knew enough about these Marine buddies to know they weren't likely to tell stories to outsiders.

They rode in silence for a while, then turned off the freeway and wound through quieter streets until Colt slowed in front of a small, well-kept house. It was the one they'd seen on Google Earth, only now the front area had been trampled on and there was yellow tape everywhere.

"This is where my brother lived," Day said, checking the address just to be sure.

"The neighbors I checked with said he's quiet but always nice. He moved in a few months ago, and from all accounts, he's liked well enough."

Day saw his brother's motorhome next to the garage. He suspected the police had been through that as well, but he didn't see any tape on it. "Let's check it out," Day suggested, and Colt pulled over.

"Are you crazy?" Knight asked. "It's a crime scene, and if we're caught messing with it, there's only so much Dimato can do to fix it."

"The motorhome isn't a crime scene." Day reached into his pocket and held out his keys. "Stephen was living the traveling life the last time I saw him, and he gave me a key."

"What do you hope to find?" Knight asked.

"Don't know. Something, anything that will tell me where he is. Now let me out."

Knight got out of the truck, and Day followed, then strode up the walk to the motorhome door. There was no tape, so he inserted the key, opened the door, then stepped up and inside.

One thing was obvious: it hadn't been used in weeks. A thin layer of dust covered the off-white counters. The upholstery was light blue, pleasing enough. Day wandered through the familiar space, feeling his brother's presence. The bed was bare, and there were no pictures or personal mementos, which had abounded the last time he'd been here.

"There's nothing here."

"Did you really think there would be?" Knight asked, and Day glared at him.

"Look at everything, remember? Leave no stone unturned. My brother lived and traveled in this motorhome for years. This was his home, though it's very different now. He's left it behind and moved on." He'd been hoping to catch a glimpse of Stephen, maybe hoping something had been left that would lead him someplace. "We might as well go." Day opened the door, glad to step out of the stifling air and into the dry heat of the Arizona sun.

"What are you doing?" an old man asked, pointing at them from next door.

"I'm his brother," Day said, holding up the keys. "I'm trying to figure out where he is."

"Clark isn't home. He hasn't been in a few days." He glared at them in that way old men sometimes had when they were looking at someone they thought was stupid. "You really shouldn't be here. If you're Clark's brother, then you should be talking to the police instead of nosing around." He turned and stomped away.

Day walked to the truck and got in, with Knight following. Colt took off, and Day stewed in the backseat, unwilling to say anything until he and Knight were alone.

The house had belonged to the Clark persona, and when he was there, Stephen had been Clark, which meant the house had to be part of his cover or whatever his false identity was up to. Day was glad he'd had the presence of mind not to use a name and let the neighbor supply that bit of information.

"Where to?" Colt asked.

"A hotel would be great."

Colt shook his head and wound back to the freeway. He sped up and went a few miles before taking an exit at dang near full speed.

"I see your driving hasn't improved much," Knight said and turned around. "When we were in Iraq on a tour, he decided to see if he could get a Humvee up onto two wheels. The asshole did it and nearly flipped the thing over."

"I did not. The wheels barely left the ground," Colt retorted.

"Not true. We were sliding toward the doors, hanging on for dear life."

Day could hear the smile in Knight's tone. Being with one of his buddies was good for him; even if Day was worried as fuck about his brother, he could see that. Sometimes you took the good with the bad.

"Is this slow enough for you?" Colt teased as he crept along, making old-lady turns until he pulled up in front of a low, sprawling house. It seemed to blend with the surrounding land instead of competing with or trying to dominate it. "My wife is a real estate agent, and she worked with an architect friend to design the place before we were married. It's sunk into the ground some." The eaves were wide, to cast long shadows, and the stucco exterior was light, to reflect the heat rather than capture it. Cactus of all kinds filled in the area in front of the house, looking perfectly at home in the surroundings.

"Colt," a woman called from the front door as they got out of the truck and Day unfolded his legs. She was pretty, darker-skinned. Day guessed she was part Native American, with jet-black hair, expressive eyes, and model-high cheekbones.

"Guys, this is Clarise," he said with a wide smile.

She hurried over to Knight and hugged him tight. "I know I still have him because of you," she said, hugging Knight again.

"This is Day, Knight's business partner, though he hasn't said exactly what kind of business they're in." Colt's steady glare told Day he was well aware of the type of jobs they had.

"It's nice to meet you," Day said and received a hug from Clarise before they were all led inside.

27

"Colt will get the bags," she said with a grin without turning around. "I made up rooms for you."

"Clarise, Day and I are here on business," Knight said. "His brother is missing, and we're trying to find out what happened to him."

She nodded. "At least stay for dinner. I called my brother, who works for Enterprise, and he's going to bring a rental car for you in a few hours."

Day had wondered why they were being picked up at the airport rather than simply getting a car, and now he understood. It was Colt's wife's way of ensuring she got to meet Knight for the first time. Listening to her and seeing the way Colt hauled in the bags and placed them off to the side in the kitchen, Day realized Colt realized she ruled the roost and was more than settled with the arrangement. Day let Knight talk with Clarise and wandered over to where Colt stood in front of the refrigerator.

"Beer?" Colt asked. He pulled open the door and handed Day one without waiting for an answer. "I was happy Knighton called. Haven't seen him since we mustered out."

"He doesn't talk much about his time in the Corps," Day said, twisting the top off the bottle.

"Nope. I don't either. Too much shit that's classified or might be classified. It's better if you keep it all to yourself. Less chance to get anyone in trouble." He pushed the door closed and took a long drink. "Knighton did save my life. That part ain't no bullshit."

"Knight's saved my life and I've saved his," Day told Colt. "But like you, it's best if we don't talk about it." He smiled.

"I guess I asked for that."

Day shrugged. "I wish I could say more. We could swap stories." Day drank his beer while Colt did the same. It seemed they both knew things about Knight that the other didn't. Neither of them could say anything, though, and if Day was right, Colt would be just as interested in hearing his stories as Day was in hearing Colt's. But it appeared they were both going to be disappointed.

"Panama was hell," Colt said and pulled open a bin next to the sink, then dropped in his empty bottle. He gazed longingly at the refrigerator and then looked away. "Clarise says I was drinking too much, and she made me promise to stop after one."

Day nodded and was tempted to offer him what was left of his bottle, but instead he drank the really fine, hoppy beer and enjoyed it.

"I heard through a friend that Knight had a hard time after his wife passed."

Day wasn't going to rise to that inquiry. "If you want my opinion, I think you should ask him. It might be good to talk over things together. Kind of help each other." On the outside Day was calm, but inside, his stomach churned, and the beer wasn't helping. He didn't want to stay here, but maybe Knight needed some time with someone who had gone through what he did.

"I may just do that if I can pry Clarise away from him."

Day drank the last of his beer. "I think I can handle that." He handed Colt the bottle. "It's the least I can do for the beer."

Colt nodded. "So tell me what's really going on with your brother. You were pretty tight-lipped in the car, and I saw the looks passing between you."

"Don't miss much, do you?"

Colt shook his head. "Never did."

"My brother's name is Stephen, and we figured out that he has an alias and that his alternate identity has a criminal record and owns the house we were at. The motorhome is the one Stephen spent years traveling the country in after I was old enough to leave for college."

"Do you think he was undercover?"

"Could be."

"And you didn't know any of this?" Colt asked.

"Nope."

"Well, I'll be damned. You see stuff like this on television." He seemed pleased. "Look, if you need anything, just holler. Things down here are pretty awesome, but we've got our share of problems, especially when it comes to the border. Guns, alcohol, drugs, people—all of it comes across in huge quantities. Those guys in the Border Patrol are doing a hell of a job, they really are, but they need more help."

"What about organized crime?"

"That's everywhere, but the border feeds it here. Lots of money to be made, and it isn't by guys working alone, but by people working together to circumvent the laws of this country and the protection of its citizens." The fire in Colt's eyes was surprising but, when Day thought about it, not unexpected. "I fought and almost died to preserve this country and our freedoms, and the criminals from the other side work to take that away from us, only they do it one drug, gun, or people run at a time."

"Colt," Clarise said as she came in the room. "Don't take Day here on one of your tirades."

"He has a point, ma'am," Day said as Clarise moved to stand right next to Colt, who calmed almost instantly just from her presence.

"I get riled up over things I can't do anything about."

"Go talk to Knight before he and Day need to leave." She had the same idea Day had, and Colt nodded to her and left the room.

Soon Knight's laugh floated in from the other room. That was always a sound Day enjoyed, but he didn't hear it often.

"Knight's good for him," Clarise said. "At least I hope to God he will be. Colt has awful dreams, wakes up screaming. I know we're keeping you from your search, but Knighton is about my last hope."

"PTSD?" Day asked.

"That and head trauma. He's so much better, but he isn't improving any longer and seems to be backpedaling because no one understands what he went through."

"Feeling sorry for himself?" Day asked, having seen the same behavior in Knight from time to time.

"Maybe a little," she agreed with a smile. "Colt's a strong man, and he hates weakness, especially in himself. So he gets upset when he wakes in the middle of the night, shaking like a leaf because there are bombs falling all around him and he doesn't know which way to turn." The concern in her eyes was genuine and warm. She clearly loved the man very much, but the strain was taking its toll; it had to be.

Day wished Knight would talk to him about what he'd gone through, but that wasn't likely to happen. Getting through Knight's Marine bastion of emotional defense was more than Day thought was ever likely to happen.

"Knight is strong too, I can see that," she continued, "and he isn't going to tell anyone his secrets lightly. You'll have to find them, dig, watch for the small signs, and piece it all together."

"Tell me about it," Day groaned and rolled his eyes.

"What are you talking about?" Colt asked when he came back into the kitchen. He looked sheepish as he grabbed two beers from the refrigerator.

Day shook his head strongly. "Not for Knight," he whispered and looked toward the other room. Knight would likely have a fit if he knew Day was interfering, but Day knew what he had gone through with alcohol.

Colt tilted his head slightly in confusion and then set both beers back in the door and grabbed a couple cans of soda.

"All right. What's going on?" Clarise asked.

Day shrugged as she pulled out a chair at the table. He sat across from her.

"You two watch each other, circling like a couple of cats ready to pounce. I understand him wanting to help you find your brother—that's the Marine in him, always up for the hunt. But the way you look out for him...."

"He's my partner," Day said. "We've spent quite a bit of time together lately, under harsh circumstances." He had to come up with an explanation that made sense; otherwise he was going to give away something he wasn't ready to share. "Knight is the biggest pain in the ass I've ever met. His capacity for assholery knows no bounds. One minute he'll be helping and the next he's off on some self-righteous crusade where he knows best." Maybe they were all like that.

Clarise chuckled and then laughed. "The crusade part sounds about right. You heard a small one."

"Hey, Day!" Knight bellowed from the other room. "Come in here now!"

Day shared a knowing glance with Clarise and followed the sound. Colt and Knight sat in the living room, which was dominated by huge leather chairs and the biggest television known to man. They were watching CNN, of all things. "What is it?"

"Coyotes," Colt said. "A band of them headed to the US were spotted and are being tracked." He reversed the live television play through his cable box and started at the beginning of the story.

"Last night the US Border Patrol picked up a band of people headed into the US. They followed them back to the border and then lost them," the announcer said and then panned to some live video. "We were able to get some exclusive video of the group of coyotes as they raced back to Mexico. However, just before they reached the border, one of the coyotes pulled a gun on another and fired. Be warned, the following images are graphic and may be disturbing for younger viewers."

The video, shot in night vision, was disturbing, and it seemed like they were right there. The man who had been shot fell backward, nearly looking straight at the camera as the momentum carried him back.

Day gasped and his hands started shaking. "Stop the picture."

Colt stilled the feed, and Day hurried closer to the screen. If the television had been smaller, he probably wouldn't have been able to tell, but this was an amazing screen and he could see his brother's face displayed prominently right in front of him.

"Is that him?" Knight asked, getting out of the chair.

"I think so," Day whimpered as he stood stock-still. "It has to be. He looks a little different, very close to the pictures of Clark Miller, but…." He watched as Colt pressed play and his brother crumpled to the ground and stayed still. "No…," Day moaned as he willed the man to get up.

The announcer cut in. "We are unable to ascertain the status of the man who was shot. Border Patrol agents are attempting to access the area in question. We will keep you informed of the latest developments."

The newscast continued with a discussion of the business of bringing people across the border and the pitfalls they faced. Day barely heard a word. He stepped back and wondered what he was going to do. His brother was his only family, and he'd been the one person Day had been able to count on when his life was at its lowest. Stephen had always been there, and Day had quite honestly felt he always would be. Stephen was his rock, his touchstone. The person he could count on for the unvarnished truth, and for love that never ended.

"What am I going to do?"

"You need to wait and see what comes of this," Knight said.

"Your brother is a coyote?" Clarise said with disbelief.

"I don't believe so." There had to be more to it than what appeared on that television screen. He knew it. There was an explanation for the second identity and what he'd just seen. The brother he knew would never profit from the misery of others.

"What can we do?" Colt asked.

"I don't know," Day said.

"We need to find out where he's been taken and if he was reached in time. If someone could film this, then they were close enough to help. We don't know how badly he was shot or if help arrived." Knight got to his feet, and within seconds he was on the phone with Dimato, explaining what they'd seen.

"I have no idea what any of this means," Day said.

Knight listened and remained silent, while Day alternated watching the television for more information and watching Knight for some sort of clue about what they should do. He got nothing on either end. Knight wandered out of the room, and Day slowly went numb with disbelief. By the time Knight returned, Day barely noticed him; he'd sat in one of the huge chairs, staring at the massive television screen.

"Dimato has no idea," Knight told him. "He said we have to wait and see."

Day turned and glared at him. "Fucking wait and see?" he asked loudly. "He expects me to sit here and 'wait and see' what the hell happened? Maybe my brother survived that and maybe he didn't. But I'm supposed to do nothing."

Knight nodded once. "That's what he said."

"Useful as tits on a boar."

When the doorbell rang, Clarise left the room and returned a few minutes later with a man. "This is my brother, Ernesto. He has your vehicle from Enterprise."

Knight shook his hand and followed him and Clarise out of the room.

Day tracked them with his eyes, his world closing in around him.

"You know this will pass," Colt said.

"My brother was just shot, and I saw it on television. He's probably dead, and he was my only family. How in the hell can that pass?"

Colt leaned forward and caught Day's gaze in one of steel. "Because it's what you have to do. If you want to know what all this is about and figure out what truly happened to your brother, then you need to push the grief, panic, and loss aside and clear your head. It's what Marines do. We have a job and that comes first. The tears come later, and yes, we all cry, though if you tell anyone I said that, I'll rip your head off."

"So what in the hell should I do?" Day asked, hardening his own gaze.

"Your job. I don't know who you work for or what it is that you really do, but I can guess. Put your mind to work unraveling this puzzle. It will give you something to do, and once you have answers, you can grieve, if that's the end result, and then move on."

"Have you moved on? It's easy for you to say that, but have you done it?"

"Yes. I've moved on, but the ghosts haven't and they never will. The doctors say they will be with me for the rest of my life. You saw what happened on television—I saw it in real life, felt it on my skin, showered the remains of my friends out of my hair and off my body. It's what warriors do, and if you want to be a warrior and run with the big boys, then that's what you're going to have to do here."

"You think I'm a warrior?" Day had never seen himself that way. He considered himself a geek more than anything.

"Knight does. When he said you would make a good Marine, that's what he meant."

Day inhaled, steeling himself against the rising grief and anger. He nodded to Colt and got a look of respect in return. Then Day stood and followed to where Knight was, outside.

"We appreciate all your help," Knight said, shaking hands with Ernesto, who then got into another car and took off.

"Where are we going?" Day asked as Colt came outside with their bags.

"To the scene of the crime, as it were." Knight turned to Colt, who nodded.

"I know that general area. It's almost due south of here." Colt set down the bags, and he and Knight began talking directions and how to get around the area. "Screw it, I'm going with you."

"You are not," Clarise said, but as soon as Colt turned to her, she shook her head, sighing softly. "I'll go get a cooler and some water. If you're going to be a damn fool, I want you to come back in one piece." She stalked back into the house.

"Don't put your relationship in jeopardy because of this," Day said.

"She's fine. If she were really angry, she never would have given up so fast." Colt pulled open the back of the rented Jeep and loaded the luggage. "I'll get my bags, and once Clarise is done mothering us, we can go."

"I'm sorry about what happened, and we'll get to the bottom of it," Knight said, his back rigid, standing tall. "Whatever is going on, we'll figure it out."

"What about the police here?"

"I'll make a few calls and see if I can learn anything," Colt said and pulled out his phone. Day didn't know who he was calling, but it seemed he was plugged in to just about everything around here. Within a few minutes, he was shaking his head. "Nothing. I called a buddy on the force. He and I did Reserves together. He said they saw the video but don't know the source or what happened to the victim." He hurried back into the house like a child racing to get a new toy.

"If we want answers to what your brother was doing and what happened, we need to go where the action is. I think that whatever happened at the house here is related to what your brother was doing out there." Knight stepped closer.

Day closed his eyes, knowing if Knight tried to comfort him at the moment, he'd break down completely, and he couldn't do that. He had a job to do, and he was damn well going to see it through. If his brother was dead, he deserved to know what happened, and whatever the truth was would come out. Whatever Stephen had been doing, good or bad, Day would learn to deal with it.

Colt returned with two bags and tossed them in the back of the Jeep. "The big one is equipment we're going to need. The border areas are rough." He said no more, and Day wondered just how much firepower they had along with them.

Clarise brought out a cooler and a case of bottled water, adding it to their growing stock of supplies. "You be careful," she scolded, then hugged Colt tight. "I know you think this is some kind of game, but it isn't."

He returned the hug and then got in the backseat, slamming the door before lowering the window. "I need to do this. I haven't felt like myself in so long."

She reached inside as Day got in the passenger seat. "I know. Just be careful and don't do anything stupid." She walked around the vehicle and spoke to Knight for a few seconds, and then she stepped back and Knight got in.

"Do you know where we need to go?" Day asked.

"Are you kidding? I used to spend two weeks in the desert down there each year. We called it survival training, but it was just time in the desert. We had plenty of supplies and all, but I know that area of the state very well."

"Is that why you have no trouble in the Middle East?" Knight asked, starting the engine.

Day was relieved. The interior had been heating by the second, and he was already sweating up a storm.

"Yeah. We used to have a ball. But I'd never let my kids do things like that. It's too lawless now. Not that it's a shooting gallery, just open space, and that's what these smugglers want. Space that's dark, loosely patrolled because resources are stretched, and where they can get in and out."

"So you can take us to where you think the shooting took place?" Day asked.

"I can get us to the general area. I know some people who can probably put us closer, if they're still there. I was friends with a lot of the desert folks when me and my friends camped out there. A lot of them have left, but I know of at least one—a guy named Grady—who should still be there." As Colt talked, he would interject a quick command to turn and then go right back to what he was saying.

"What kind of person lives alone in the middle of the desert? Not that I'm judging, just curious," Day inquired.

"People who want to be left alone. There are amazing folks out there, and then there are some cuckoo types. A group of people went out there a while ago on some religious quest, spending forty days in the wilderness… most of them are still there because they were never found. Wasn't much left of those who were."

"Day, the desert is beautiful—rugged, peaceful, sparse, yet full of life if you know where to look," Knight said as he followed Colt's continued directions. "A lot of people see nothing but brown upon brown, but there are birds, insects, cacti, and a lot of small animals. Life feeds on life out there. It's unforgiving and treacherous. So stay close and listen to Colt and me. We have experience with this."

"Fine," he said, turning away from the others, folding his arms over his chest, and trying not to sink into his own muddled thoughts. "Hey!" he growled when Colt smacked him lightly on the side of the head.

"No thinking like that. You don't know what happened, and you have to put those fears out of your mind."

"Yeah," Day groaned, wiping his head. "But why'd you hit me?"

"Distraction," Colt said. "Take this exit and follow the road south," he said to Knight. "There's going to be a turnoff in about fifty miles or so that we need to take. There used to be cacti on either side of the turn, and if they haven't been stolen, they'd be a good marker."

"Stolen?" Day asked.

"That's another thing out here. Poachers. With the push for sustainable landscapes, there's a demand for exotic species. Some cacti live for decades, and poachers go into the desert to dig them up. The fines are huge if they're caught, but the rewards are big as well."

"Jesus."

"We're heading into no-man's-land, where might makes right and the winner is the guy with the biggest and fastest gun," Knight said. He glanced at Colt and explained, "Day can shoot."

Day opened his mouth to say he could more than shoot, but Knight stilled him with a chilling look. Day had once beaten Knight in a shooting contest, which had dented Knight's pride.

"Good. I'll show you how to load and use what I brought."

Day nodded and kept quiet. He was a crack shot with pinpoint accuracy with most firearms, and he doubted there was much Colt could throw at him that he hadn't seen. But Knight seemed to want him to keep that to himself, so he went with it.

The road started off decent. At least it was paved. But the conditions got worse as they went along, with potholes increasing in size and number. Day tried to keep his mind on the task at hand and did a remarkable job. It took all his self-control not to play the image of the shooting in his head over and over again.

"What did you and your brother do for fun?" Colt asked.

"Stephen bought me my first skateboard. My mom and dad were less than thrilled, but he showed me how to use it, and soon I was doing jumps and curls. That is, until I fell and gashed my arm. Stephen took me to Mom, who scolded him something awful, and I got an earful the entire ride to the hospital." Day turned back to Colt. "Of course, I got right back on the skateboard as soon as I got home. Gave my mom a heart attack, but Stephen was right there, cheering me on." Day curled his lips upward. "He was always there. I remember when he went away to college. It felt like the house was completely empty. He was so much older, and no one would have blamed him for not wanting his little brother around. Stephen had included me in a lot of things, so when he was gone, I felt like the life had left the house." Day turned back to stare at the desert, with its hills, sand, and scrub plants stretching as far as the eye could see. "The life truly did leave the house when Mom and Dad were killed."

"Stephen took care of you then," Colt said.

Day shook his head. "Stephen gave up his life for me. He had dreams that he put on hold so he could raise me. I owe so much to him." Day tried not to think about the very real possibility that Stephen was dead, but he failed. He'd seen the video, knew they were in the middle of nowhere, and it was likely that even if help arrived, they would be too late. Just because he didn't have an official answer from someone didn't mean his brother wasn't dead already.

"Don't make Colt hit you again," Knight said with surprising gentleness as the road got worse and the Jeep bounced even more.

Day ground his teeth but kept the anger that wanted to well up from exploding outward. "Go to hell and drive," he muttered and turned away, staring out at the desert bleakness. Yes, he knew the desert had its own majesty and beauty, but at the moment, all he could see was monochrome, because that was how he felt. He didn't want to see anything else, so as far as he was concerned, it wasn't there. All Day wanted to do was get the hell out to where his brother had been to see the place, to try to find out the truth and where his brother was. Nothing else fucking mattered.

Knight sped up and the Jeep rocked and lurched, but Knight didn't let up. Day turned, watching the cloud of dust fill the air behind them with a plume of brown. More brown; everything was brown. He didn't care how much time had passed, just that they kept moving.

"The turnoff is right up ahead around a bend," Colt said, and Knight slowed.

The cacti were still there, and the Jeep passed them as Knight made the turn and then sped up. The land grew flatter and the road rougher, but Knight kept going, and the cloud of sand behind them grew and followed.

"Keep an eye out. You're likely to see anything out here. The last time I was this way, I came across someone who had crossed the border. I'm guessing the coyotes ran or they got left behind. There wasn't much left by the time I found him."

"What did you do?" Day asked.

"Made an anonymous tip and moved on. Life is harsh out here, and unfortunately, to the coyotes, it's only worth the amount they're paid. Not a penny more. And they get their pay in advance." Colt sat back, and they all grew quiet as Knight continued their trek farther and farther from civilization.

Minutes ticked by, turning to an hour with no one saying anything. That was fine with Day. He spent the time gripping the "oh shit" handle. Being in mortal fear for his life had one advantage: he didn't have time to worry about anything other than Knight's driving.

"We're coming up on Grady's place," Colt said. "Slow down and take it easy."

A low building appeared on the horizon. It looked like a small compound, and as they approached, a house, pens, and small corrals became clear.

As Knight pulled to a stop, an old man of about sixty, with a beard and white hair and holding a gun, strode toward the Jeep. "I have nothing you want, so get the hell out of here," he called, raising the gun.

"Grady, it's Colt." He lowered the window. "Put the dang gun away before you shoot yourself."

Grady laughed and lowered the rifle. "What in Sam Hill are you doing here?" He walked toward the Jeep, and Colt opened the door and got out. "This ain't a good place for anyone with any sense. I lost mine years ago, and no asshole coyotes and smugglers are going to run me off."

"This is an old Marine buddy, Knighton, and a friend. You still got satellite?"

"Yeah," Grady said. "Don't watch it much. Ain't nothing on but crap."

"You watch the news?"

Grady grunted. "You must think I'm daft, boy. Of course I do." He narrowed his gaze at both him and Knight. "This got to do with that shooting they caught on film?"

"We think the guy who got shot was Day's brother. We couldn't find out anything, so we thought we'd try to see what we could dig up, and you were our first stop."

"Well, come on in. If'n we're gonna jaw, we might as well do it civilized." He turned away, and Day opened his door and stepped out. Knight did the same, and the three of them walked up a dirt path to the door. Indoors, it was surprisingly cool. "I got panels out back for 'lectricity and to pump water. I run it through the house and then out to the goats. Keeps things really nice, even in the summer, when it's hell on earth out there."

"You build this all yourself?" Day asked.

"Sure did," Grady said proudly, and Day took a minute to look around. The furniture was ancient, worn, and patched. The walls held skulls, lots of them, in all different sizes. It was cool, in a creepy sort of way.

"It's nice," Day said.

"It's a shack, but it's home and it's mine. I came out here to hunt for gold. Didn't find any. But then I hit something more precious out here. I decided to dig and found water. So I raise the goats and other things, hunt some, and shoot trespassers." He grinned, showing where a few teeth had once been.

"Grady, have you heard anything about the shooting?" Colt asked.

"Nope. Only what I saw on the TV."

"Damn, we were hoping to get there."

Grady chuffed. "What do you think I am, a fool? I know this desert like the back of my hand. To you city boys, it all looks alike."

"I have to admit you're right about that," Knight agreed, and Day nodded.

"To me... I know right where they were at. Saw that big rock outcropping when they panned out. You got a map?" Grady asked, sitting at a table made of wood that seemed as old as himself.

"In the Jeep," Knight said and left, giving Day a chance to look around some more.

"You know, the workmanship is incredible." He knew to compliment someone on their home.

"My father was a carpenter, and he taught me the tricks of his trade," Grady answered. "It ain't much, but it's home." That seemed to be something he said when he didn't have anything else to say.

Knight returned and handed Grady a map. Day wondered for a second where it had come from, but figured Colt must have given it to Knight. "We're here, correct?" Knight asked, pointing.

"Yeah, and here is the outcropping. It's only about twenty miles or so, but it's off-road and going to be hard. You need to be careful. The land is pretty flat, but there are tracks and such. Those are used by law enforcement and the coyotes they chase." Grady looked up from the map, turning to Colt. "What do you boys hope to find?" He turned to Knight and then to Day. "You'd be best to turn around and go back to the city. That is a crap place, and anyone you meet you have to consider hostile."

"We need to find out what happened to my brother. I don't care if it's coyotes, Border Patrol, local law, or drug smugglers." Day drilled his gaze into Grady. "Someone out there knows what the fuck happened, and I'm going to find out if I have to kick the ass of every piece of shit from here to the Mexican border. I could sit in Phoenix and wonder what happened or go out there and find out."

"You know, sometimes it's better not to know," Grady said.

Day wondered if he was right, but he turned to Knight, silently asking him the same question, and knew by the flash of pain in his eyes that it wasn't. "And sometimes not knowing will rip your heart apart and work at your soul," Day countered.

Grady was silent for a few seconds. "Can't argue with that neither." He turned to Colt. "You boys need any supplies?"

"Clarise made sure we have enough food and water to last a month, but I appreciate the offer. Is there anything you need?"

"I'd kill for a good beer," Grady said, and Colt went out to the truck, then returned with a couple of cans, already cold. Grady grinned and popped one open, making a satisfied sigh that resounded through the room. "Stop on your way back if you come this way."

"We will, and thank you," Colt said, glancing at them and motioning with his head toward the door. "You be safe."

They all shook Grady's hand, thanked him for the help, and then went out to the Jeep.

Knight started the engine and pulled away as soon as they were inside. "Okay, what's the real deal? There were a few goats, but not enough to support anyone for long."

"Everyone out here does what they have to, to survive. I don't know for sure, but I suspect Grady's working with someone."

"You mean like coyotes?" Day asked.

Colt sighed. "Sometimes I like to think that things are black-and-white. Immigrants are bad and all that. But the truth is that they have to be pretty desperate to try to make the crossing through the desert here. So I think Grady provides a safe place if needed. Especially for people who are abandoned. If they make it to him, he tries to help. I've never seen it, but I've heard stories. Even the coyotes respect him."

"Then that's good, I guess."

"It is. The real problem is a patchwork of crap laws that don't work and make everyone do shit that could be done faster and better if there was a clear, concise program."

"Okay. So do you think the information he gave us is correct, or did he send us on a wild goose chase?" Knight asked.

"I'd like to think he told us the truth, and what he said jibes with what I know, so I say we go for it. I don't think he'd purposely put us in harm's way, but he also isn't going to jeopardize the people he works with."

"Huh," Day mumbled. "Things are not as they appear."

"They rarely are," Colt and Knight said at the same time.

They headed out into the desert as the shadows began to lengthen. "We aren't going to make it before nightfall," Knight said, turning to Colt as he slowed. "We really should have thought this through."

"No worries. I have blankets with my gear, and we can put the seats flat. I can sleep anywhere, so…."

"Sleep out here?" Day asked. "What if someone comes?"

"Then either Knight or I will wake and shoot if we have to. Right here should be a good place to stop. We're still far enough from the border that we should be left alone."

"Okay," Knight said, pulling to a stop. "I say we get set up with what little light we have left, eat, and then hunker down for the night. No lights, no fire, and no drawing attention to ourselves, and we should be left alone."

Just what Day wanted, to be in the middle of nowhere the night after his brother might have been killed and God knows what was out there waiting for them to go to sleep before swooping in for the kill. Maybe that would be preferable to waking up to find out his brother was gone.

Colt got out, and Day followed and helped him get his equipment out of the back. He put the seats down, and Colt threw in a few blankets. "It's going to be a long night."

"I have no doubt of that," Day said as he laid out the bedding and made the bed up as best he could.

"You don't mind sharing with Knight, do you?" Colt asked.

"I've shared more than the back of a Jeep with Knight." Day turned away, hoping he wasn't giving away too much. "This will be fine."

"Should we keep watch?" Knight asked.

"If you actually think I'm going to sleep out here…," Colt said. "I haven't slept through the night in months. I'll take the first watch and wake you if I need you."

The sun set and the last of the light faded from the sky. They ate dinner, such as it was. Afterward, Day walked around the Jeep and sat on the still-warm hood, looking up at the sky as the stars multiplied by the second. He said nothing, listening as Knight and Colt talked softly. He could hear their voices, but not what they were saying, which was fine. They had things to talk about, and Day stared at the constellations with tears running down his cheeks. He didn't make a sound; he couldn't. If he opened his mouth, the wail of grief would well from inside and burst out of him.

"Day," Knight whispered from next to him. The darkness had fallen around them so deeply, he couldn't see him at all, and yet he knew exactly where Knight was. "What's going on?"

Day opened his mouth, but nothing came out. He wanted to tell Knight that Stephen was the one who had taken him out into the middle of nowhere when he'd had a project on stars at school. He couldn't tell him that Stephen had shown him Orion and Cassiopeia, as well as the big and little bears. He couldn't see them all now, but he knew where they were. Day closed his eyes, unable to look at the stars any longer.

A hand touched his shoulder, and the Jeep shifted under him. Then Knight settled next to him. He was there, with just that small touch. It was like Knight understood what he felt and how alone he'd been.

"Stephen taught me the constellations. He had a telescope, and he used to take me out so we could look up at the sky. Once he found Jupiter so I could see the great red spot, and then he located Saturn so I could see the rings."

"Is there anything you and Stephen didn't do together?"

Day shrugged before remembering Knight couldn't see him. "After Mom and Dad died, Stephen took over everything. If I had a project at school, he didn't help me do it, but he provided as much information or experience as he could to help me. If I had astronomy assignments, he took me stargazing. After I was bullied, he got me into karate class and took it with me so I could defend myself. He never did things for me, but he made sure I learned everything I could."

"Sounds like your brother was pretty amazing," Colt said in a low voice as he joined them.

"He was." Day wasn't sure if Stephen was dead, but he already missed him.

"So what in the hell was he doing out here? This is the domain of the lawless, and that doesn't sound like your brother. What isn't adding up?"

"That's what we're here to find out," Knight said.

"Stephen had to be out here trying to help people. That's the kind of man he was. He wasn't a coyote or making money off human trafficking. He was here to do good—I know it." Day had to believe that. He had no other choice. All his memories, and a good part of the man he was, depended on it.

He stopped talking and chanced a look up at the sky once more. A streak of light zoomed across the sky, burning brightly and then flaming out.

"Shooting star," Colt said, and Day didn't correct him. "I used to sit in a foxhole—it was pitch-black, like this—and I'd scan the sky for them."

"You too?" Knight asked.

"Yeah. It was always 'hurry up and wait' with hours of doing nothing, so at night I looked up and watched. Sometimes I'd see ten or twelve in an hour."

Day didn't feel like talking any longer. He lay back, staring upward. He felt Knight slide off and heard Colt move away, their footsteps quietly receding, leaving him alone. "Knight," Day whispered and expected an answer, but heard nothing. He didn't move, watching, trying not to sink into the aching despair that loomed around the edges of his being, trying to muscle closer and closer to the present.

He must have dozed off, because he woke as the chill of the desert night began to creep through him.

"Are you feeling any better?" Knight asked from next to him. "You were snoring."

"I don't know what I'm supposed to feel. Stephen is dead—he has to be, based on what I saw." He sat up and turned toward Knight's voice. "You said once that you thought it might be best to leave what happened to Cheryl and Zachary in the past. Do you really believe that? Does walking away seem like a more attractive option than searching for what happened?" He stared into the darkness, trying to see enough to gauge Knight's response. But with no moon and the absence of any other light, the effort was futile.

Knight sighed, but he didn't say anything.

Day turned toward the sound and waited nervously.

"I don't know what's better, okay?" Knight finally said. "Sometimes I think I should let Cheryl and Zachary go and be at peace, and then I hate myself because I'm not avenging them."

"Like you're letting them go instead of finding out why they were killed?"

"I hate not knowing," Knight said. He didn't raise his voice, but the tension was there nonetheless.

"If someone hurt Clarise, I'd hunt them down to the ends of the earth, and with my last breath, shot and bleeding out, I'd kill them. No price is too big to make right when someone you love is taken from you."

Day admired the unwavering devotion and firmness in Colt's voice. He didn't know what to say and waited for Knight's reaction. What he got was the wind blowing across the land around them, whistling in his ears.

"That's—" Day began, but Colt shushed him. He wished to hell he could see something, anything, but with only the stars and no other light, it was hard for him to see his hand in front of his face.

"Listen," Colt breathed, almost too faintly to be heard.

Knight touched his shoulder, hopefully as reassurance, but Day wasn't sure. At the moment all he could hear was his heart pounding in his ears as he strained to catch whatever it was that Colt had heard. Then a flash, not much brighter than a star, but much closer to the ground, caught his eye a distance away. He stared at the spot, willing it to repeat. A few minutes later it did, farther away, like a twinkling star.

Then a cry went up—a wild dog, calling to its mate, echoing over the land.

Colt grabbed the front of Day's shirt, tugging him forward and down to the ground. He sat still as the cool night air slunk under his clothes. Day knew Knight wouldn't feel the cold at all. "That was no dog," Colt whispered. "That was a coyote calling to the people they're guiding. This one is very skilled at hiding."

"What do we do? Catch him and see what he can tell us?"

"No," Knight breathed directly into his ear.

"These guys are too independent. He might know, but he isn't going to tell us anything. As soon as we get close, he'll disappear, leaving the people with him to fend for themselves."

That seemed opposite to the attitude Colt had had at his house.

"These guys are territorial and have their own routes and ways of evading the authorities. We're too far away from the guys who might know about your brother. But tomorrow night? That's a completely different story. For now we stay quiet and let them pass." Colt sat down; Day heard a slight scraping of the ground and nothing more.

They all gathered without making a sound. At least Colt and Knight did. Day couldn't even hear their breathing and wondered if they'd snuck off. His eyes had gotten used to the ultralow light, so by angling his head, he could see their forms against the stars.

"They're far enough away now that we don't have to worry," Colt said after an hour. Day hadn't heard anything more, and he'd seen no further flashes.

"My God," he muttered. "How far do they have to walk?"

"Phoenix, maybe farther. It depends if the coyote has transportation, and then it can be tricky. They will walk for miles and hide if they hear anyone." Colt got up. "I'm going to stay up and watch, so you two should get some sleep."

He opened the back of the Jeep. He wasn't going to argue with Colt. He needed some time to think. Grief was closing in. He'd heard what Colt and Knight had told him about fear and nerve, but it was becoming impossible for him not to think that his entire family was now gone in the time it had taken a gunman to pull the trigger.

He climbed in the back, his head just touching the back of the front seat. He had to pull his legs in a little in order to fit. The liftgate was closed, and Day was alone inside the vehicle. He certainly wasn't going to ask Knight to join him. He couldn't hear any voices outside and didn't hazard a look. There wasn't much he could see anyway.

Day lay alone with his thoughts and fears, wondering if he was going to make it through the night with his sanity and emotions intact. The longer he was alone, the closer he got to the precipice. Over and over, he played the image of his brother being shot through his mind: the most minute movement, the step back, the way he fell, clutching his chest, then the slight bounce when he hit the ground. There was no way on earth his brother could be alive. The constant slow-motion replay told him that.

The door opened, and Day turned out of habit. Colt had removed the bulb from the inside dome light while they'd been driving, so they were left in darkness. Knight climbed in next to him, his scent unmistakable, stretched across him to close the door, apologized under his breath, and then lay down. Day turned away, closed his eyes, and stilled. He didn't want to say anything.

Knight didn't move either and then sighed. Day nearly did the same as the Jeep rocked slightly. He felt Knight roll over, and then Knight lightly rested his hand on his hip. It stayed there, unmoving. He didn't say a word; words weren't needed. Day knew Knight was there and understood. That was enough. Part of him wanted to be held and told everything would be okay, but the larger piece was happy with the silent, stoic show of solidarity. Knight, of all people, knew exactly how he felt.

"Go to sleep," Knight whispered.

"I don't think I can. What happens if…." Day wasn't sure exactly what he was afraid of.

"The mind does what it wants. Our dreams are the one thing that can take us places we only wonder at, but they have a mind of their own. I spent years trying to drink my dreams away. If I got drunk enough, then they couldn't touch me because I was numb. I tried again and again, failing each time. Drinking didn't keep the nightmares away. It only added to them and took them over."

"Do you still want to drink?"

Knight moved closer, his warmth spreading across Day's backside, keeping the chill from the desert night at bay. Day had always thought of Arizona as being hot, but especially in the winter, there was nothing to hold the heat in once the sun had set. "Every single day."

"Then why not drink?" Day asked.

"Because as much as I want a drink, there are things I'm beginning to realize that I want more. I want a normal life where I can remember what happened the night before. I need to deal with the loss of Cheryl and Zachary rather than running away from it." Knight squeezed slightly, massaging Day's hip.

Day hoped he was one of the things Knight wanted more than alcohol, but he didn't want to press it. Things with Knight seemed fragile at the moment. They were in a decent place. At least they weren't sniping

48

at each other constantly. That could change. Hell, maybe if they were snarking, he'd know things were okay and the way they'd always been.

"I can hear you thinking, and you aren't helping yourself. Hopefully tomorrow we'll be able to find some answers."

Day rolled over. "Do you really think coming out here is going to make a bit of difference? Shouldn't we have stayed in town and gone to the authorities to see what information they have? I mean, this seems like a long way to come to try to find a spot that we may or may not be able to actually locate from a video." Day wasn't seeing the logic in all this.

"Someone working out here knows where that video was filmed, and they know why the shooting took place. All we need to do is find that person. These guys are like drug runners. They have their territories, and they'll kill or run off anyone who doesn't work with them. So it makes sense that if we can get into the territory, we'll find the men from the same organization."

"What if we do and they don't want to talk?"

"We aren't a government agency, and I dare anyone to withstand what Colt can do to them or threaten to do to them."

"But there was a body in Stephen's house. Shouldn't we be worried about her?"

"We can't get anywhere near that. Unlike in movies, if we set foot near the house, we'll be corrupting a crime scene, and the police won't hesitate to charge us and bring us in. Besides, I know in my gut that we're on the right trail. There's a reason Stephen was shot, and the source of that reason isn't in Phoenix. It's out here. Sometimes you have to go with your gut, and it's telling me that the reason for the second identity, for his being shot, and where he is now are all out here."

"So what are we supposed to do? Sit tight, hope that someone comes by, the way they did tonight, and then get them to talk to us?"

"Yup. That's pretty much the plan. Now go to sleep. You're going to want to be rested and alert tomorrow." Knight sighed. "I wish to hell we had some of that communications equipment we had before. It would be nice not to have to rely solely on the satellite phone."

"It is what it is." Day knew he was largely useless on a mission like this. His specialty was communications. He was a geek at heart. Sure, he could take care of himself, but Knight and Colt were the real experts on this recon stuff.

"Exactly. So don't think too much about it. Close your eyes, let the worry go, and will your body to calm."

"I can't do that. You can fall asleep anywhere, but I can't."

"Then think of this. It's nine at night, but for us it's eleven and we've been up for hours and flown cross-country and are now in the middle of nowhere. If you want to be useful and not put yourself or us in danger, close your eyes and go to sleep. I'll be right here, and I'm not going to let anything happen to you."

Knight's gentle tone, without a hint of sarcasm or exasperation, settled him. There was nothing he could do about what had happened except find out what he could, and to do that, he had to be at his best. Day closed his eyes and tried to still the movie that threatened to play.

"Just let it go," Knight whispered. "I'm here and Colt is outside. No one is going to harm you, and we're going to get all the answers we need. Relax and slip off into sleep." He sounded like he was speaking a child's lullaby.

Day sighed and did what Knight told him to. He didn't think of anything other than the voice from the man he'd come to trust with his life. He rolled back over, and Knight slowly rubbed up and down his back. Day counted the rubs to give his wandering mind something to do, but he didn't reach ten.

Chapter 4

KNIGHT WAS already awake and had gotten out of the Jeep before the first rays of sun struck it. He knew from experience that within seconds the inside of the vehicle would become a mini oven. He figured he'd let Day sleep a little longer. Day had tossed and turned for most of the night, sometimes making whimpers of fear, or maybe pain. Knight heard each one and wished there was something he could do to make it better. Understanding what Day was going through and being able to do something about it were very different things.

"See anything?" Colt asked from where he sat on a small scrap of tan blanket with his back to the medium-brown Jeep exterior.

"No. Was there anything in the night?" Knight asked.

"No. It was quiet after our little excitement. But we should get out of here as fast as possible. There are granola bars in my bag and yogurt packs in the cooler." Colt stood, and Knight stared at the horizon, where the sun was strengthening, getting ready to pop up over the horizon. "He going to be all right?" Colt asked, peering inside the Jeep.

"Yes," Knight answered.

Colt met his gaze. "After what he saw yesterday, no one would blame him. We've seen strong men go to pieces. There's no shame in it."

"No, there isn't, but he's stronger than you give him credit for. He's surprised me at almost every turn since I met him." Knight smiled. "Would you believe he saved a kid who was being shaken down and in the process took on two gang members?"

Colt cocked his eyebrows slightly, and Knight nodded.

"He can take care of himself."

"Yeah, but you know being able to defend yourself is very different from being able to handle the emotional barrage something like this brings."

"Tell me about it," Knight groaned, and Colt tilted his head questioningly and then nodded. The sun rose, sending cactus shadows

51

skittering across the desert floor. Heat began to build almost instantly, and Knight unlatched the liftgate.

Day sat up, blinking, looking like he'd been dragged through hell.

"We're leaving in fifteen," Colt said. "So clean up, eat, change clothes, and we'll get the hell out of here."

"Did you sleep?" Day asked.

"Some," Knight fibbed. He'd slept very little, with Day's distress bringing his own to the front once again. "You heard him, and he means it. So get moving." They needed action and tasks if they were going to hold it together.

Day slid out of the Jeep, grabbed his bag from the front seat, and walked around to the front. Knight got his bag and did his best not to watch as Day stripped off to change clothes. Knight changed as well, and he caught Day watching him in return. He instantly glanced at Colt, who was busy shoving half a granola bar into his mouth. The other half followed within seconds.

"I see your table manners haven't improved," Knight said.

Colt flipped him the bird as Knight pulled on his shirt.

Colt tossed each of them a bar and a bottle of water. "Eat a yogurt and anything else in there. The cold isn't going to last much longer." They finished eating, policed the area, and then jammed their bags in the back, climbed in, and took off.

"I'm glad we filled up at that last station," Knight said.

"There's one about forty miles on the other side of where we're going." Colt leaned over behind him to look at the gauge. "We should be all right as long as we aren't stupid."

They went slow over the rough terrain. After an hour, Colt pointed to a small outcropping rising in the distance. "That was on the film for just a few seconds, so it's got to be in that area. I think we need to head to the east side and start there. The angle should be close."

"Hope like hell this isn't a wild goose chase," Day grumbled.

Knight glanced at Colt, who nodded. Knight thought maybe Colt's prediction earlier was coming true. "Watch for tracks and things. People came through here recently."

Day nodded and stared silently out the window. "I can see the way you're looking at me, and I'm fine. When the time comes, I'll be ready to go."

"How do you know?" Knight asked. "You never know when the time will come." He stared over at Day, slowing the Jeep.

"I saved your ass more than once, and I can take care of myself," Day snapped. "And you fucking know it."

"Head over there," Colt pointed, and Knight continued driving as carefully as he could. The rustle of papers sounded from the backseat. "There's an arroyo over there, and it's going to cut us off after a little bit. Head south so we can get closer. Then we'll need to walk."

Knight had seen terrain like this before and knew how to distinguish subtle differences in color and texture.

Day practically had his face pressed to the glass. "How can you see anything? It all looks the same. We're going to get lost and never find our way out."

"It isn't the same," Knight said. "The rocks are slightly darker, and see the angle up there? The shadow on the ground over there is where the arroyo has cut through. It's the drop-off, and why we couldn't continue after dark. If you can't see it, you can't avoid it." Knight pulled to a stop with the Jeep in a slight depression to help camouflage it.

"I'm taking a GPS reading," Colt said as he got out. "We aren't going to be able to see our location very well on our way back."

While he took the readings, Knight got a small pack out of his case and filled it with food and water. "Drink your fill," he told Day. "Hydration is the name of the game out here."

"How long will it take, do you think?"

"Somewhere between a few hours and never. But we have to stay after dark if we want to intercept the coyotes," Colt explained as he filled a pack as well. "Let's get going. We can jaw on the way." He closed the doors and locked the vehicle, and then Knight hoisted the pack onto his back and started walking.

Day fell in behind him, and Colt brought up the rear. "Why do you think we're going to meet anyone tonight? Wouldn't they stay away after what happened?"

"Nope. Tonight is the last night of the new moon cycle. It will be a sliver," Knight said. "Once the moon gets brighter, there's more light and it's easier to see and be seen out here. They're going to use darkness as much as they can to try to bring people across."

"No border runs, no money," Colt added flatly.

"Okay," Day said, his water bottle crinkling as he finished it.

Knight turned, took the empty bottle, and shoved it into the pack.

They continued walking, avoiding cacti and as much rough ground as possible. They had to cross the washout and had difficulty getting up the other side. The walls were steep and smooth. Eventually they found a spot to climb, but not after going some distance out of their way. Once all three of them were up the other side, they continued toward the outcropping.

"What's this?" Day asked, stopping to look at something shiny in the sand.

"Don't," Colt warned, grabbing his hand. "They set traps out here. The coyotes know where they are and can avoid them or lure the Border Patrol into them."

Knight stopped, looking around while Day and Colt stepped around the area. Then Colt picked up a rock and tossed it over. Spikes sprung out of the ground, jabbing at the empty air near where Day had been standing when he'd bent down.

"Keep a look out," Knight said, slowing his pace, knowing a trap could take any of them out of commission.

The heat was building, and even though it was December, the sun was still strong. Knight sweated quite a bit. He made sure everyone drank plenty and was thankful they had a lot of water. The outcropping grew gradually larger until they stood next to it. "I'm going to climb up and see what I can," he said, handing his pack to Day before exploring until he found a foothold. The outcropping was slanted, like the earth had turned the rock on its side eons ago. He climbed the low end and found a path that led upward. It had been traveled recently. If he were a coyote, this would make a great lookout post.

He expected the area to be deserted during the day.

"Don't fucking move," a rough voice said from behind him just as Knight was approaching the summit.

Knight groaned and stopped, holding out his hands. He cursed on the inside, knowing he should have been more careful. "I'm not armed," he said, turning slowly to face a short man of Mexican descent with a round face, missing teeth, and scraggly hair and clothes. "Do you live out here?"

"*Sí*, gringo, this is my summer home," he said with a grin, "and you stepped into a trap you ain't going to get out of."

"I wouldn't be so sure of that," Colt said as he stepped up behind the man, cocking his gun. "So, Pedro, you put your gun down."

The man slowly set his rifle on the ground and turned toward Colt while Knight retrieved the weapon and groaned at himself for being a fool.

"What you gringos want?" the man asked.

"Information," Colt answered, but the man shook his head.

"I tell you nothing."

Colt took a step closer. "You'll tell me whatever I want to know or I'll shoot you in the knees and let the scavengers finish you off."

"You don't have to waste the bullets," Day said, coming up behind Colt. "I can break his knees, and then if he doesn't talk, I'll jam his nose up into his skull. The fucker will know he's going to die, and he'll feel every ounce of pain." Day searched the man and came up with two knives, which Knight took. "I'd like to take a shot at this guy." Anger rolled off him in waves like hot air currents.

Knight liked seeing the fear in the man's eyes.

"I don't know anything."

"You know plenty," Colt said. "Now tell us about the man who was shot."

"You police?" he asked.

"Worse," Knight said. "Guns for hire, and the man killed had important friends."

The man swore steadily in Spanish. Knight didn't need a translation.

"We could just kill him now and move on, wait for his friends," Knight said to Day and Colt.

"We were told to leave no one we found alive," Colt said, and Knight was glad Colt had picked up on the game.

"I want to do it," Day said. "I'll make it really painful."

All of them were up to speed, and the guy was practically shaking. Whatever organization controlled this area, this guy was most likely a low-level set of eyes and nothing more. "I know nothing."

"You keep saying that, but my friend here speaks Spanish, and all your swearing tells us something different. Now sit. We're going to have a talk." Knight motioned with the gun, and the man sat on the ground like his one leg was stiff. Knight could use that if necessary. "We want to know about the man who was shot."

"You his friends, so you know enough."

"Answers like that will get your knees broken," Knight said, turning to Day. "His right leg is already hurting. Tweak it good. Let's hear him scream."

"No, no, I tell you. I no shoot him. I hear it from here." He pointed. "It happen there. I just stay up here and watch. They say he was a... mole? He work for government. So he had to die."

"What happened to him?" Colt demanded.

"I no know," he answered, glancing at Day and shaking a little. Day's expression was as hard as Knight had ever seen it. "I tell the truth. I hear shot, and they tell me what happen and that I stay to watch, see who come."

Knight shared a glance with Colt and Day. "They say who shot him?"

He shook his head.

Knight wasn't sure they were going to get any additional information out of him. He was just as scared of the people he worked with as he was of them. If he said anything, he was certainly dead.

"What do we do with him?" Day asked.

"His cave is there," Colt said. "See what's inside."

Day walked over and returned with some old rope. "He's got plenty of supplies. Looks like a mini 7-Eleven in there."

"Tie him up inside, and his friends can set him loose when they come through tonight, if they find him." Colt kept his gun ready while Day tied the man up and deposited him on the floor of the cave.

Knight made sure he wasn't going anywhere, then left the cave and continued to the top of the outcropping to look around.

"What do you think?" Day asked.

"Colt, do you want to stay with our friend? I'll take Day over to check out his story and see if we can find anything where he said the shooting took place. We'll be back in an hour, and we can wait out the day here. If they have lookouts, they're planning to come back through here, and I want to be ready when they do."

"I got things here," Colt said, and Knight led Day back down the path to the ground and then out to where the man had indicated.

"There were plenty of people through here," Knight said, reading the ground around him. "A group must have come through here last night." He led on, following the trail backward to a tangle of footsteps in a small clearing surrounded by cactus and dry sagebrush. The ground was stirred up, but Knight wasn't sure why.

"Is this the place?" Day asked reverently, looking all around, walking the edges. "It could be from the video, but it's hard to tell."

"I don't know. The tracks led here, but that just means people came through this way. I don't see any blood or stained ground." Knight carefully bent and a glint caught his eye. "What's this?" he asked softly. He thought it might be another trap and stepped back, tossing a rock the way Colt had, but nothing happened. Knight did it again and then cautiously went closer. He leaned down and picked up a small piece of brass. "A bullet casing," Knight said, showing it to Day. "Whoever was here didn't police his brasses and left us this little gift." He got a plastic bag from the pack and slid it inside. "I don't know what good it will do us, but it's something."

Day nodded.

"Don't move," Knight snapped, and Day stilled. "Retrace your steps out of the area." He knelt to try to see any minute changes in the contour of the land. Closing his eyes and using the place where he'd found the shell as a reference, Knight tried to imagine where the players would have stood and made his way over in his mind. He moved slowly and opened his eyes, looking down at a flat spot. "This is where he fell, I think. In the video, he was about fifteen feet from the shooter, which would put him about here." There was no blood or discoloration. "The helicopter that took the video would have stirred up a lot of dust, depending on how close they were, and after the shot, everyone would have scattered and run like hell, if they hadn't fled before."

"So you think this is it?"

"Yeah, but where's the blood?" Knight asked.

"Maybe someone covered it over, or his clothes soaked most of it up," Day suggested, kneeling on the ground, placing his hand on the place where his brother had fallen. "What I want to know is what happened to him." He lifted his gaze. "I don't know what I expected—maybe to still find his body."

"Border Patrol should have been out here," Knight said. "This shooting was on the news, nearly live."

"But what if they weren't? What if the news guys were out here on a tip of their own and got the film?"

"Border Patrol would still investigate. It was a shooting, after all." Something wasn't adding up.

"Maybe they couldn't find the place, and the news organization wouldn't tell them where they were to protect a source or something."

"If we can find it, so can they." Knight stood. "This stinks of something, and I'm not sure what." Knight stilled, thinking. He ran through what they knew and could draw only one conclusion. "I'm betting your brother was working with Border Patrol. That's the only thing that makes sense. He was undercover or something."

"That would explain why he was shot, but…."

Knight inhaled deeply and hesitated. The thought that raced through his mind was a solid possibility, but he hesitated because he didn't want to give Day false hope.

"Just fucking say it," Day demanded.

"What if he really wasn't hurt? It was dark as hell out here, and the pictures we watched were with night vision. What if your brother wore a vest and was shot, went down, and then got out of there when everyone scattered? It's possible."

"Yeah," Day said with an uptick in his voice.

"It's a possibility and no more. It fits what we know, but so does the fact that your brother was a coyote, and they shot him for another reason and took the body."

Day shivered in the heat. "Up and down, hope and crash."

"I know."

Day stepped back, and Knight continued examining the ground for anything it could tell them. But he'd gotten what he could from the area.

"I keep wondering what the person killed in Stephen's house has to do with all this," Day said once Knight was done.

"I understand. But we need to keep our eyes on the prize. The people in the neighborhood said that your brother wasn't there at the time of the murder. So it isn't likely he's a suspect. What you said you wanted was to find your brother, and we tracked him here. Now we need to figure where he could have gone or been taken from here, and if he's still alive."

Day nodded and began pacing a small area. "If he's dead, then he's dead and I need to accept that and let law enforcement handle it. However, if he's alive and survived that shot, then he had help from somewhere."

"So where does the trail lead?" Knight prompted and waited.

"Border Patrol?" Day asked.

Knight nodded. "If he's dead and the coyotes took his body, we aren't going to find it. They buried him somewhere out in this desert and that's the end of it. The trail is gone, and we might get lucky and find someone who knows, but basically everyone is going to close their mouths and hightail it across the border." Knight sighed at the pained look on Day's face. He hated going over these options, but it had to be said. "So let's work under the assumption that he's alive."

"I like that," Day said nervously.

"He was shot at pretty close range, and there's no blood, so if he is alive, then he was wearing a bulletproof vest. Maybe the whole scene with the shooting and even the video itself were all part of some bigger plan."

"What should we do?" Day asked hurriedly and with energy in his voice that had been absent for a while.

"We continue our plan: see if we can learn anything tonight and then get the hell back to Phoenix tomorrow and camp out at Border Patrol. And see if Dimato can put pressure on them to give us some answers. There are still some questions we need answers to."

"All right, let's go," Day said, and Knight gathered up their things, leaving nothing to let anyone know they'd been there, and then they started back toward the outcropping.

The heat continued to build. The temperature wasn't all that high, but there was no relief from the sun. They drank water and ate some more as they walked. Knight was grateful for a little shade once they reached the outcropping.

Colt met them at the base.

"What about our friend?"

"There was some liquor in the cave, so he and I decided to have a few drinks while you were gone. I only appeared to drink, and he drank enough tequila that he isn't going anywhere for quite a while." Colt chuckled. "Did you find anything?"

"A casing and the location of the shooting. No blood, though. Not a drop," Knight explained.

"So the whole thing was a put-up job?"

"That's possible. We're going to hang out and try to get some answers tonight. Then tomorrow we head back and speak to Border Patrol."

"What should we do in the meantime?"

"I say we hang out here," Knight said. "There are lots of supplies, and since…"

"His name's Juan," Colt supplied.

"…Juan's initial greeting was so nice, we'll take advantage of what he's got and arrange a surprise for anyone coming by in the night."

KNIGHT UNDERSTOOD and had long accepted the "hurry up and wait" attitude that military work demanded, and this was no exception. They walked the top of the outcropping, exploring it thoroughly while at the same time staying out of sight as much as possible.

Juan came to as the sun began to set and seemed to have one hell of a headache. He groaned whenever he moved, and his eyes lacked focus. By the time it was fully dark, Juan was gagged and tied in the cave with Day.

Knight and Colt lay on the cooling rock, looking out over the land for any sign of visitors.

"I checked Juan's pockets again," Day said as he approached from behind.

"You should be with Juan," Knight scolded.

"Then you don't want the codes and the light he used to signal that the coast is clear? Fine, I'll go back." Day pressed the light into Knight's hand. "Good luck."

"Is he always like that?" Colt asked. "What's the code?"

"They'll flash three times, and he needs to answer with two flashes if it's clear. Otherwise they assume there's trouble," Day whispered. Knight figured Day had already returned to the cave, but he obviously hadn't, and Knight sighed as Day's footsteps got softer.

"I should have checked him out."

"Neither of us thought about it. We'd searched him earlier, but were looking for weapons."

"Yeah, but it was still a rookie mistake, and one I'm sure Day isn't going to let either of us forget," Colt groused.

"You can say that again." Knight knew this would be brought up every time he questioned Day, most likely for years.

They grew quiet, watching, waiting, and listening. The hours ticked by slowly. He'd been trained to be patient, but bloody hell, maybe he was getting too old for this.

Colt shifted next to him every few minutes. "Fuck," he breathed, and Knight nodded in the darkness. "I hate getting older. Maybe Clarise is right and I need to stop acting like a young buck."

A light flashed on the horizon. It was so fast, Knight nearly missed it. Two more quickly followed, and he flashed the light he had twice.

"Now it gets interesting."

They waited as voices approached where they lay in wait. Someone called in Spanish, and Knight turned to Colt. "Get Day, now." He waited once again while Colt hurried away.

Another soft call went up, and Day answered. Then nothing.

"What did they ask?"

"If the supplies were ready."

That made sense. They couldn't bring over everything they needed with them, so the coyotes had someone—in this case Juan—hide on the outcropping with the supplies until they were needed. What he didn't understand was how the supplies and Juan could be here if Border Patrol had been through the area, and they had to have been, with a shooting on television. Something else that didn't add up.

"We need everything, big group, lots of money," a man said in English, obviously calling up to Juan, who wasn't going to answer. "You awake?"

"Sí," Day called, and Knight tensed. He waited, pressed to the ground, until he heard someone climbing up. Once he saw a figure against the stars, he held his gun level and waited until a light shone in his direction.

"I think you're looking in the wrong place." Knight leveled the gun, ready to shoot if the man opened his mouth. "I suggest you keep quiet and sit down or I'll blow your head off."

The man nodded.

"Are you alone or is there another coyote with you?" Knight asked. "I heard you speak English, so don't play dumb."

The man held still.

"Call your friend and say nothing else."

"Javier," he said, and soon another man joined them.

Colt appeared from near the cave.

"We're going to have a little talk," Knight said. Both men's eyes became as wide as saucers, filling with fear.

"What do you want? Money?"

"Information," Knight answered. "I want to know about the shooting last night."

"We know nothing," the first man answered.

"Then I'll shoot you both for being stupid," Knight said flatly. He was getting tired of being out here, and dealing with these people was getting on his nerves. "I'm not going to interfere with your business or what you're doing. You and the people you're with can continue right on once I get some answers. I want to know about the man who was shot, and I know you know about it."

They looked at each other. "We no shoot him."

"Who did?" Knight pressed.

"Rodriguez. He crazy," the second man answered. "The... boss, he not happy about it." The first man knocked shoulders with the other, most likely to shut him up. "Rodriguez no come back anymore."

"Was he killed?" Neither answered, but they became even more agitated, so Knight figured he had his answer. "Why did Rodriguez shoot him?"

"They never like each other," the second man said.

"Did someone order it?" Knight asked, moving closer.

They both shook their heads.

"What happened to the body?"

They each looked at each other rather blankly and then straight back at Knight.

"I think you can do better than that."

"We don't know. Last we saw, he was dead right over there. Now the body gone. Maybe it get eaten."

"Or maybe it was taken away," Day accused and stepped forward. There wasn't enough light to see much, but Day's movement caught Knight's eye and then the man went down onto his back with a thud. "I want to know what happened to him."

"We don't know. Rodriguez said he was undercover. Clark help us a lot, but now they say he was a traitor. A fed or something," the man on his back groaned. "Rodriguez shoot him and now he dead too."

Day stepped back and let the man get to his feet. "I want answers."

"We know nothing. He was here, he got shot, and now he gone. That's what we know."

"Did someone take the body back?"

"No. It was where it fell," the second man answered. "We answer. Can we go now?"

Knight nodded. "Slowly and make no fast movements. You can take Juan with you. He's probably tired of our company by now."

Colt brought out Juan and untied him, then let him join the others. "Take what you need and go. Make sure the people with you get where they're going in one piece. And then I suggest you find yourselves a different line of work. The trail of immigration through this area is closed. Be sure to tell your boss that. We intend to make sure that everyone here knows what's going on, and after the shooting, this is going to become a very busy place."

They nodded, then grabbed the supplies Juan had been watching and took off like scared rabbits.

"Do you think they were telling the truth?"

"I think they were taken off guard and were about ready to piss themselves. But yeah, for the most part. What they said corroborates what we found. And if the shooter has been eliminated, then that avenue of inquiry is cut off."

"Where do we go from here?" Colt asked.

"You go back to Phoenix and go home. Day and I pay a visit to Border Patrol and try to get some answers from them. They have to know more than they've been telling the media. If anyone has an inkling of what's going on out here, it's them."

"Are you sure?"

"Yeah. Let's hunker down for the night, stay on watch, and then get the hell out of here tomorrow. We found out what fucking little there was out here, and now we have to see what other leaves we can shake from the trees. Day's brother is somewhere. He didn't just disappear, and while we know more than we did, we still have almost as many questions as when we started this little trip."

KNIGHT HALF expected more visitors in the night, figuring the guys they'd gotten the better of might return, but it was quiet. In the morning they drove to the nearest gas station, an old, rundown place that looked like something out of an old movie—a cheap slasher movie, to be precise. Thankfully they had fuel, and once the tank was filled, they continued back to Phoenix.

Day was quiet the entire way.

Knight didn't want to admit it to himself, and he'd never say it out loud, but he was fucking worried. Day always talked, and he gave him shit about something, anything… all the damn time. Hell, Knight sometimes gave him stuff to give him shit about. Getting a rise out of Day was fun. But this was scary. He'd seen it before with guys in combat when they lost their best friend, the guy they relied on. Those sorts of relationships weren't easy to replace. Knight knew that. He was honest enough to admit that when he'd lost that person in his life, he'd crawled into a fucking bottle for two years and still hadn't managed to get completely out of it.

"We'll find him," Knight told Day, who either ignored him or didn't hear what he'd said. He chanced a glance at Colt, who nodded once, watching the back of Day's head.

Finally Day turned toward him, and Knight's stomach clenched at the blankness in his eyes. Day was fiery; it was part of what Knight liked about him. But now there was none of that fire he'd first seen in Mexico or the determination to see things through that had come forward in Europe. Day had turned into a rock or he'd shown his inner strength at those times. Now it seemed used up.

"So," Knight began, clamping his eyes closed for a split second before plowing on. "You going to talk or go all pussy on me?"

"Fuck off!" Day growled, their usual answer to questions they didn't want to respond to.

Knight had no intention of backing down. "You fuck off. I thought you had what it took to do this job. It turns out you don't have the backbone or the guts. Things get tough and you back away, shut down, and try to will it all away." He glanced at Day and pressed on. "All that shit that happened in Mexico, the bullet you took, the steel you showed in Europe. Was that just luck or a front to cover for being a chickenshit pussy?" He kept his voice as harsh as he possibly could.

"Knight, that's not fair," Colt said.

"The hell it isn't! Look at him. Acting like the fucking world's come to an end."

"Well, maybe mine did!" Day yelled.

"Yeah? What the fuck are you going to do about it?" Knight challenged. "I told you once that you would have made a hell of a Marine. Was I wrong? Was the strength I saw just luck or the last of what you had?"

"Jesus," Colt said, and Knight turned, steeling him with as cold a glare as he could. Colt put his hands in the air and sat back, shaking his head.

Knight pulled off the road and to a stop. "Was I wrong?" he demanded.

"The hell you were. I bested you in a shooting contest that you fucking challenged me to, and I saved your skin. It's you who can't deal with shit, and all that 'what happens on the ship, stays on the ship' shit you pulled. So don't talk to me about being a pussy. You can't even deal with your own fucking feelings. So I'm having a little trouble dealing with the fact that my brother is most likely dead. I don't know where the hell he is and may never fucking know. You deal with your own shit, and let me deal with mine!"

Knight glared at Day. Yeah, he'd poked the bear on purpose, trying to get a rise out of him. But he hadn't expected Day to throw that up at him or to bring up what they'd had together in front of Colt. "So you're saying you have what it takes?" Knight countered, ignoring the part where Day might have just outed them a little. If he showed no reaction, maybe Colt wouldn't pick up on it.

"Of course I do, you ass," Day countered.

"Then prove it," Knight snapped firmly. "We're on a job, an assignment, and no matter what our personal feelings and worries are, we have to put them aside. Any Marine would tell you to man up, put aside your personal shit, and do your job. The lives of the rest of the people around you could depend on it."

"Fine," Day retorted with the tone of a petulant child, but Knight didn't fail to notice Day sat taller in his seat and looked around rather than staring blankly. "What's the plan from here, oh mighty know-it-all?" The sarcasm was back—that was also a good sign.

"We get back to Phoenix and start digging. You brought a computer, and I say we use the information we have to dig into everything we can. It's what you're really good at it, so use those skills to try to find your brother."

Knight pulled back onto the road and then pressed the accelerator to the floor. They needed rest, showers, and food. Then maybe they could think more clearly.

TWO HOURS and many miles later, they dropped Colt off at his home, said good-bye, thanked him for his help, and returned Clarise's cooler. Knight half expected Colt to ask to stay with them, but as soon as he saw Colt and Clarise together, he knew Colt had done what he could, but it was time for him to return to his happy life.

Clarise sent Colt into the house with a smile and then rapped on the window, and Knight lowered it. "Thank you. He's longed for some sort of action for a while. Now I hope it's out of his system." She smiled, and Day lightened up and smiled back.

"I hope he got what he wanted," Day said.

"Oh, he did." She stepped back, and Knight raised the window. She waved and went inside as Knight pulled away, intending to find a hotel downtown.

"What did she mean?" Day asked.

"Retirement has been hard on Colt, so she let him have a taste of what he was missing in the hope that he'd realize just how good he had it at home. And I think that's exactly what happened."

Day nodded, and Knight headed toward the freeway.

"You know you're a complete and total asshole," Day said.

"That's what you keep telling me." Knight merged into traffic toward the center of town.

"God, sometimes I just hate you." There was no heat in Day's voice. "You said all that shit to make me angry and get my mind off my brother and onto the task at hand."

"I don't lie."

"No. But sometimes you're a bull in a china shop. Never talk about feelings or anything gentle. Just turn into a bulldozer and mow down everything in your path in order to get what you want."

Knight changed lanes, sped up, and then grinned at Day. "I usually get what I want with a minimum of mouth from you, so I'd say my methods are successful. And if you don't mind my saying, your head seems to be back in the game, rather than stuck twenty feet up your ass and in a spiral of misery. So yeah, score one for me."

"Bastard," Day growled.

"Pussy," Knight said without losing his grin.

"Fuckhead," Day countered.

"Pain in the ass."

"Asshole."

"Dick."

"Jarhead."

"Yup, and proud of it." Knight waited for Day's comeback, but all he got was a groan. "I win."

67

"Maybe, but you're still an asshole." Day didn't turn away as they approached the downtown business district.

"Like I said. Not only can I live with that, but you thinking I'm an asshole seems to be normal, so maybe I'm doing something right."

"Where are we going?"

"Hotel, then the federal building. We have some folks at Border Patrol to talk to and try to intimidate. I'm willing to bet they have information we need, and they aren't going to part with it just by asking."

"So how do we get it?"

Knight exited and came to a stop at the end of the ramp.

"You don't know, do you?" Day pressed.

"Don't have a clue. I'm the bull, remember? You're the one who usually finesses things. So I was counting on you to think of some way to sweet-talk them." Knight made the turn, and Day grew quiet while he thought. Knight pulled into the Hilton Garden Inn parking lot, found a place, and then got out, waiting to see just what Day would come up with.

They got their luggage and had reached the front door of the hotel before Day finally spoke. "Why don't we try something really innovative—the truth, or at least a version of the truth—and let's see what that gets us."

AFTER RESTING a little and making some calls to report back on what they'd found, they walked into the federal building and up to the offices of Border Patrol.

Day spoke to the receptionist, flashing a smile Knight hadn't seen since they left Milwaukee. "I'm looking for my brother, and I think someone in your office might know where he is or at least what he's been doing for you."

"What's your brother's name?"

"Stephen Ingram," Day said, and she typed into her computer.

"I'm sorry."

"Try Clark Miller," Day said, and she stared at him but did as he asked.

"We don't have either person working here."

"Actually we've found out that they're two names for the same person, and we believe someone here is aware of it and knows what happened to him. So I suspect you should kick this inquiry up the ladder and see if that gets some action. Otherwise we can go to the news media. They're in a frenzy over the man who was shot on television."

Knight drew himself to his full height. "Please do as he says," he commanded firmly in his best no-nonsense tone.

She nodded and picked up the phone. "I have two men out here who are asking about a Stephen Ingram and a Clark Miller." She listened. "Yes. They say they are the same person, whatever that means." She nodded once. "Yes." She hung up. "Someone will be with you in a minute."

"I bet they will." Day didn't make any motion to sit, and Knight stood right behind him, just off to the side. He loved that Day wasn't backing down.

"Can I help you gentlemen?" a middle-aged man in a crisp suit asked as he stepped into the lobby.

"I'm looking for my brother. I saw him shot on television."

"I'm sorry, but…."

"You don't understand. I know someone created a fake identity for him, and when we went to where he was shot, there was no blood and no body. So I'm wondering what you know about all this, considering this activity took place in your area and under your nose. Now, we can continue investigating and make the news media aware of what we found, or you can stop playing dumb and tell me what I want to know about my brother." Day seemed ready to snap at any second. Knight wasn't sure if that was part of the act or not. Either way, it was very effective, judging by the beads of sweat on the man's forehead.

"I think you'd better come with me," he said nervously. He met the gaze of the receptionist, and a soft buzzing signaled the door had been unlocked for them. He pulled it open and led Knight and Day out of the lobby and into a conference room just beyond the door. Day went inside and then whirled around, arms crossed over his chest.

"I want some answers," Day said firmly. "But first I want to know who the hell you are."

"Simon Craft, and you're on my turf, so I'll be asking the questions."

"Well, Simon. If you want to walk out of here in one piece and without being covered in bruises or worse, I think you're going to need to start coming up with some answers that make sense," Knight growled. "This is Dayton Ingram. He's Stephen Ingram's—aka Clark Miller's—brother. Now either you're completely incompetent at what you do and have absolutely no idea what's going on down at the border, or your agency is involved in whatever Stephen was doing."

"I think I'd better have your name as well," Simon said.

"Knighton." It was his turn to fold his arms over his chest.

"Knighton what?" Simon demanded.

He reached into his wallet, pulled out a card, and handed to Simon. "That's all you need to know. Just call this number, and you'll get the information you're permitted to have."

"Why don't you both have a seat?" Simon motioned to the chairs. "Please remain here while I make some calls."

Dayton pulled out his phone. "I suggest you don't take too long, or we'll begin making some calls of our own, and whatever cell phone jamming system you have in this building isn't going to do crap with this."

Simon blanched slightly and left the room. The door closed, and Knight figured Craft would post men outside the door. "You did really well." Knight paced the room, staring up at the camera in the corner. He grinned and nodded.

Day pulled out another device from his pocket and turned it on. "This should jam anything they have listening to us," Day said. "I know Simon knows something. I can see it in his eyes."

"Yeah. He's as jumpy as a long-tailed cat in a room full of rocking chairs. I figure Simon is either changing his shirt or his shorts before he makes that call."

"Dimato?"

"Yup. Who else?" Knight smiled. "I can't wait until he gets back."

It took Simon less than five minutes, and he was indeed wearing a fresh shirt. "It seems you two are known for making quite an impression," Simon commented as he closed the door.

"I take it you got what you needed?" Knight said. "Now we need you to tell us what the hell is going on. We've been trailing Ingram's brother for the past few days. We went out to where he was 'shot,' and there was no blood and no body. We also know it's likely the Clark Miller alias was created by someone in law enforcement, given the characteristics of the identity...." Knight figured he had to give something to get something.

"All right, please sit down and I'll tell you what I can."

Day pulled out a chair, and Knight sat next to him, letting Simon sit across from them.

Simon drummed his fingers on the table. "Your brother was working with us and has been for the last six years or so."

"Why?"

"Stephen has been with Border Patrol, going around the country, scouting out scams. He's a troubleshooter of sorts. When things heated up down here early last year, we brought him in and he went undercover. We set him up. The Clark Miller alias had some history, and it worked for him, so we used it. Had him buy a house he couldn't afford on paper, all that, so he'd look desperate. He was able to get into one of the crews and began working his way into one of the organizations."

"Let me guess," Knight interrupted. "He was getting really close, and just as you were getting ready to swoop in and pick them all up, everything went to hell."

"Yup. He saw they were getting suspicious and starting to question him. We figured his cover has been compromised in some way and arranged to get him out of there."

"Then a dead person shows up at his house? Do you know who she is? He'd told Day there was someone he was seeing."

"We aren't aware of anyone in his life," Simon told them. "The girl is most likely someone that Carlos Sanchez wanted to send a message to. We figure he placed her at Stephen's to kill two birds with one stone."

"Jesus," Knight groaned.

"Who's Sanchez?" Day asked.

"The guy is into everything," Knight said, turning to Day. "Drugs, girls, illegals, booze—anything he can make a buck at. He runs everything from Mexico, where he owns most everything and everyone. He's untouchable."

"And we were getting close," Simon told them. "Because of Stephen."

"So was he really shot?" Day asked.

"He wasn't supposed to be. He was wearing a superthin vest that should have stopped the bullet. It was dark, and there was supposed to be plenty of chaos. After the dramatic footage, Stephen was supposed to have been able to use the cover of night to get back here. We'd announce the death of a former drifter, Clark Miller, on the news and that would be that."

"What happened?"

"We don't know. He hasn't shown up yet, and like you said, there was no body. It seems that Stephen has disappeared completely, and we're at a loss. When you came in here, we were hoping he might have contacted you. Obviously he hasn't done that either."

"No," Day said in that defeated tone Knight had heard in the car. He couldn't pull the act again like he'd done then. It had worked, though, and Day was holding up amazingly well under the circumstances.

"Then why the stall?" Knight demanded. He knew the toll this was taking on Day, and blast it to hell, he hated that more than if it were happening to himself. Day didn't deserve this; no one did. And to top it off, they had been without much sleep for two days, and his patience was wearing paper-thin. Taking out a bureaucrat wasn't going to help that, but damn, it might make him feel better. Knight smiled icily and cracked his knuckles to accentuate his point.

"We're trying to find him, and if you leave a number, we'll call you if we learn anything new," Simon told them.

Knight shook his head. There had to be more than that.

"I have authorizations just like everyone else, and that is all I can give you," Simon added with a slight pleading in his voice. "I have a brother, and I know how I'd feel if I was in your situation, but there's only so much I can do. I will help if I can, and I'll call if we hear anything, but we're afraid he's out of our jurisdiction."

"Have you called in some help?"

Simon swallowed and hesitated. "I can't tell you that at the moment. But I will say," he said as he turned to Day, "your brother has helped this agency and his country a great deal. We owe it to him to find out what happened and to bring him back safely. I intend to see to it that this agency fulfills that obligation."

The man had fire from somewhere. Knight wasn't ready to believe him fully, but it didn't seem like an act.

"All right," Knight said when Day nodded. He gave Simon his cell number. "Call if you have anything, and we'll return the courtesy. If you work with us, we'll work with you." Knight tapped Day on the shoulder, and they got to their feet.

"Where will you be?"

"For now, the hotel," Knight answered, and they left the room, with Simon escorting them out to the lobby. They shook hands, and then Knight called for the elevator and they rode down to the ground level and headed to the car. Conversation was at a minimum as Knight drove them back to the Hilton Garden Inn. They needed somewhere with comfortable beds, room service, and a staff that would leave them alone.

Knight paid his usual attention to what was happening around him, leading a nearly catatonic Day up to the room. He had never been so happy to get behind the locked door of a hotel room in his life. "Go take a shower. I'll order food. Once we clean up and eat, we can sleep."

Day nodded and went into the bathroom. The water started and ran steadily.

Knight set the bags on the stand and ordered a huge amount of food. He noticed, once he ordered the food, that the sound of the water never changed.

Knight went to the bathroom door, listened, and then cracked it open. Day stood in the tub with the curtain pulled partway, leaning against the tile wall without moving. Knight thought he might have fallen asleep, but then he saw his eyes were open. *Shit.* Knight shut the door and took off his clothes, then got under the water with him and pulled the curtain closed.

"It's all right," he said, remembering the last time he'd done something like this. It hadn't been in the shower, but in the sand, after the battle was over. It was quiet and a friend had had too much. Marines were tough, there was no doubt about it, but they were also human and sometimes something snapped. "You don't have to say anything, but know I'm here." Knight pressed against him, his own body reacting to the proximity even if he had no intention of acting on it at a time like this. He always reacted to Day. That had become the one predictable thing between them after all these weeks. This man acted on him in a way no one else did. Knight grabbed some shampoo and gently rubbed it into Day's hair, caressing him, then rinsed it out.

"How do you do this? How did you last after…?" Day asked after a few minutes. "The fear of being alone is enough to swallow me whole."

"I didn't last," Knight admitted. "I tried to escape for a long time." The grief for Cheryl and Zachary melded with what Day was feeling. "But there's hope for you. They said that the shooting was a put-up job. He wasn't really shot, which we thought was the case. We were right, and now we need to try to find him before Sanchez does. You need to concentrate on that and let the rest go. I know they scared the hell out of you and everything that's gone on has messed with your head, but it isn't real."

Day turned around. "The hell it wasn't." He nearly slipped, and Knight caught him, holding Day up against him. "I saw him shot. That makes it real."

"Think of that as a movie. It was an act, something meant to convince someone that Stephen had been eliminated. What we can hope is that it worked and Stephen's disappearance is part of his plan to stay alive. We don't know what's going on, and I don't think Simon knows it all either." Knight touched Day's chin. "Remember the leak we had to plug a few weeks ago? What if they have one here? Sanchez isn't without a lot of resources. So maybe Stephen disappeared on his own."

Day released a huge breath, settling against him. Damned if Knight didn't love the feel of Day against his skin. Knight held him closer, letting the water course over them.

After a few minutes, he grabbed the soap and began washing Day's heated skin. "Just let it go for now. I know it seems impossible, but you can tell your body and mind to do anything. I can sleep at a moment's notice and push ideas away when I have to. It's something you learn, and I know you can do it too."

"How?" Day breathed.

"Think of something you want more. There's always something more important. In battle, guys make it through because of their families or their fiancée—someone they love and care for more than anyone else. The man in battle who is the most dangerous and unpredictable is the one with nothing to live for. Then he has no grounding and will do something no one expects. Sometimes those people win Medals of Honor, but often they get themselves and maybe someone else killed. You need to concentrate on what you have, what you can hold on to, in order to help you get through this."

Day locked their gazes. "What did you hold on to?"

"Zachary," Knight answered. "I always held on to him. He was close to my heart… always."

Day nodded. "When we were under fire, I held on to Stephen." He tightened his grip. "I think I need to hold on to you now."

Knight would let Day hold him as long as he wanted. He soaped his hands and slicked them down Day's broad back and then over the curve of his smooth ass. "How about if we hold on to each other." Knight shifted his hips, pressing them to Day's, his cock sliding alongside Day's, eliciting a soft groan that resonated in the enclosed space. Knight got more soap, then pressed his hands to Day's chest, stroking in small circles, bumping his fingers over Day's nipples.

"Jesus," Day whispered, closing his eyes.

"I know. Let's get you clean and fed."

Day shook his head. "I need…."

The rest of his words trailed off, but Knight got the idea. He knew what Day wanted. He turned Day around and pressed him to the tile wall, hands flat against it. He slid down his back, licking warm, wet skin until he parted Day's cheeks, diving in as though he were a buffet. Day's scent and taste filled his mouth, earthy, slightly sweet, sending desire coursing through him. Knight wanted this man, this single person, more than he'd ever wanted anyone in his life, and that single fact scared him more than being shot at or finding himself on the receiving end of shell fire. He'd already lost those closest to him, and he couldn't go through it again. But the sounds Day made for him drove him onward. Taste, scent, energy, need—he had to have Day. Without him there was nothing at all.

"Knight," Day groaned, pulling him back out of the pit of his worries. He moaned and pressed his tongue deep, taking his own advice and letting it go, giving himself over to what was more important. "Please make me forget."

"I will," Knight said, standing back up and pushing the curtain aside. He stepped out and raced into the other room, dripping on the carpet. He found his bag and tore out a condom from his kit. He slammed the bathroom door and nearly tore the shower curtain away in his haste to get back. Day's eyes were wide, but he hadn't moved, and Knight moved right up behind him, pulling Day until they were chest to back. He carded his fingers through Day's wet hair. "I need you too."

"Then take me," Day groaned.

Knight nearly dropped the condom packet but managed to get it open. His hands shook with excitement. "It's been too long."

"Whose fault is that? You get close and then back away again." Day turned around and lunged at him, slamming their bodies together so hard, Knight nearly lost his balance. He clutched at Day, dropping the condom and not caring. Their mouths came together in a kiss that drew blood and had Knight seeing red—not from anger but from sheer, all-consuming passion. He needed Day so badly he couldn't think straight, just like Day clung to him, needing him.

"I can't let go," Knight said even as Day pulled away and turned off the water. He half stumbled out of the shower, grabbing a towel. Day wiped off most of the water, and Knight did the same, dabbing the fabric without taking his eyes off Day.

He dropped the towel, took Day's hand, then opened the door, and stepped over his clothes and the things he'd scattered on the floor in his haste. He grabbed another condom and pushed Day down onto the bed. He let the condom drop and leaned over his luminescent lover. He didn't really glow, but that was how Knight saw Day, especially when he was like this. The two of them fought sometimes and argued a lot, but there was nothing more beautiful in the world than when Day looked up at him, eyes filled with passion, wanting him, needing his touch. Knight's heart grew larger each time it happened, and more than once he'd wondered if his heart was too small for this man.

Day pulled him down into a kiss, hard and demanding, while he wrapped his legs around Knight's waist, tightening them to communicate that he wasn't going anywhere.

Somehow Knight found the condom, and when they broke the kiss, he managed to roll it on before returning to the kiss. He entered Day's heat as slowly as he could, pressure surrounding him. Day gasped and held him tighter as their bodies connected. Knight had never considered himself romantic. He loved, and when he did, it was with all he had, just like he did everything else, but romance hadn't been in his repertoire until now. Knight pulled away, watching Day's gleaming eyes as he sank deeper.

When he stopped, Day clenched around his cock, gripping him, holding him in place.

"Is this okay?" he asked.

Day smacked his shoulder. "Fuck me," he mouthed.

"I won't hurt you," Knight told him.

"You haven't so far," Day said. "Now stop treating me like I'm made of glass."

Knight pulled away and slammed into Day, both of them groaning. Every time he withdrew, Day drew him back. He needed him, and hell if he knew why. Day moaned and grabbed Knight's hips, pulling him forward.

"Bossy bottom," Knight said.

"You should know by now that I'm bossy all the time. It's one of the things we have in common. We both like to be in control of everything."

Knight grabbed Day's arms and pulled them away, then moved his hands up over Day's head. "Right now, I'm in charge, and I think you need it that way." He growled, lips right next to Day's. "There are times when it's tiring always being the one everyone expects to have the answers and make the decisions. Sometimes it's nice, especially in the hands of someone you trust, to just let go, and that's what I want you to do. Let go of everything for a few minutes. Put yourself in my hands. You were willing to do that a few minutes ago, so do it now."

Day nodded, his gaze never wavering.

Fuck, that was hot, and Knight moved faster, listening for the hitches in Day's breathing. Moans and gasps came fast and furious, Knight delighting in each one, changing angles until Day's eyes became unfocused and rolled in his head. That was a beautiful sight. Day was flying. Knight had seen that look before, and he'd heard his shallow breathing. Knight released Day's hands, caressing his chest and sides. He wanted as much sensation for Day as possible.

"I can't take much more of this," Day gasped.

Knight trailed his right hand down Day's belly and gripped his thick cock, stroking him hard. He didn't want Day to last. He needed him to come unglued.

"Oh shit," Day swore, quivering like a leaf in the wind.

"I've seen many things in my life, but none of them was more beautiful than you are right now. The energy, the gleam in your eyes, the way your lips curl just so when…." He changed angles again and heard the hitch in Day's voice as he dragged his cock over Day's spot. He was fast approaching the point of no return, so Knight gripped Day's cock hard, stroking firmly, loving the steady stream of expletives as Day gripped him harder.

Day stilled, closing his eyes as he came with a shout. Knight continued stroking, unable to control his own body any longer. Day's climax pulled his own out of him, and Knight filled the condom, shaking uncontrollably. Then he stilled and let the warmth of afterglow settle on both of them. He loved the floating perfection where nothing could touch him and his mind was free, if only for a few seconds.

A knock on the door drew Knight back to himself. He groaned and lifted himself away, regretting the second their bodies disconnected. He stepped into his pants and opened the door just a slit.

"Room service."

"Thanks," Knight said, cracking the door just enough to take the tray. He brought it inside, signed the slip, and returned it to the waiter. He wasn't going to let him in the room or even see inside. Day still lay on the bed, and he was his. No one was going to see or disturb Day. "I added a tip for you."

The young man looked at the slip, smiling. "Thanks so much." He turned and hurried back down the hall before Knight went inside.

"Come on. I know you want to sleep, but we need to eat first." Knight helped Day up and then to one of the chairs at the table. He set the tray in the center and began parceling out the food. "I got us steaks. I figured after two days of granola bars and beef jerky, we deserved something good."

Day moved slowly, cut his meat, and started to eat. "God, that's good."

"I know, isn't it?" Knight ate and enjoyed the view of Day naked across from him. "We should eat more meals with you naked. It really adds to the taste of the food." He was salivating and it had nothing at all to do with the steak.

"Where are we going to go from here? We have to find Stephen," Day said as he continued to eat.

"I don't know. Neither of us is thinking clearly at the moment. So after the food, we sleep and then put our heads together. There's probably some clue or piece of information that we have that we haven't thought about."

Day nodded and yawned. "I think you're right."

"We've been running on energy and adrenaline for hours now. Finish eating and we'll get some sleep for a few hours." Knight returned to his food, his own thoughts a jumbled mess that he hoped rest would clarify, but he wasn't particularly hopeful. "I'm not the kind of guy who talks a lot about his feelings." The thought came out of the blue, and he didn't have enough sense to stop it.

"You think I don't know that? You don't talk about very much in general."

He thought he'd done plenty of talking.

"I think the time is coming when you need to tell me what happened in Panama," Day said between chews before gulping down half a glass of water.

"I can't," Knight said. "I'll never be able to tell anyone about that, ever. It's sealed so tightly it can never come out. None of it. That's the shit part of it. The only ones I can talk to about it are the ones who were there, and if I do, then I tell them the ultimate result of that mission, and that I can't do." Knight set down his fork and pushed back from the table. "I know now that I paid a terrible price for that action, but I didn't know that then or until a few weeks ago. I went through hell, but I can't put them through that same hell, and I will if I say something." Knight stood and grabbed his glass of water, wishing it were vodka to dull the pain that was building quickly. In the last few weeks, he hadn't wanted a drink more than he did at this moment.

"Then tell me about it."

Knight shook his head. "You already know enough to be dangerous just because you know there's something there." He walked back toward the bed. "You need to promise me that you won't look into this. I know you have amazing skills, and if you wanted to, you could find the information, especially if you looked in the right places or talked to the right people. Please don't do that. Panama was a mistake, and it's cost way too many people too much. That has to end."

"So you're going to let it go and walk away from the man who killed Cheryl?"

"No," Knight said firmly. "But I have to do this my way. The person behind their deaths has made mistakes, and information has come into our possession about him. Not enough to identify him, but we know he's out there. And if we know he's there, unless we're careful, he might know that we know."

"So you want me to keep my head low, don't do anything to alert whoever this is, and wait?" Day asked, pushing back his plate.

"Yes. That's what we have to do." Knight sat on the edge of the bed. "I never talk about this with anyone."

Day nodded and walked over to him. "I know you don't, and I know what you saying something means." Day sat next to him, taking his hand. "For someone who rarely talks about his feelings, you have a way of expressing yourself that makes how you feel perfectly clear."

Knight nodded and sighed. "I think we'd better get some sleep so we can get our minds back on the task at hand. The past will stay where it belongs for a while." He hoped. He had found that his past tended to rise up and color everything in his life. "We have to find your brother, and that's all that's important at the moment."

Knight stood and walked back to the table, piled the dishes on the tray, and placed it out in the hall. Then he put the Do Not Disturb sign on the door, slipped off his pants, and climbed into bed.

Day made sure that the curtains were closed, blocking out nearly all the light from the outside. Then Day climbed into bed and moved right next to him. "I think we both need some time to clear our heads."

Knight couldn't agree more and closed his eyes, willing his body to sleep.

Chapter 5

DAY HAD no idea how long they slept. He was comfortable, and for the moment, his head was quiet. "Knight."

"Yeah, I'm awake," Knight said, but neither of them moved.

"We'd better get up and figure out what we're going to do." Day reached over to the nightstand to check his phone. There were no messages or calls. Not that he'd expected any, but he kept checking just in case. "I feel better but could probably sleep for hours more."

"I know," Knight groaned as he rolled over, the bedding slipping away. Day couldn't help watching. He'd seen him many times and felt him skin to skin, but somehow he never got enough.

"We need to figure what our next move is."

"I was thinking while I was waiting for you to wake up." Knight cocked his eyebrow slightly. "You know your brother better than anyone. If he'd pulled off this fake and made the people after him think he was dead, then where would he go?"

Day shrugged. "I wish I knew. When we were kids, Stephen always had a place of his own. He used to build forts in the backyard with strange entrances and trapdoors. There was one where we had to pull a special lever that would unlock the door, but inside there was a mechanism that required a combination. Once he put that in, the actual door could be opened, and that one required a ladder because it was up under the eaves."

"Okay. So would he have created a safe room of sorts at his house?"

"He might, but he hasn't lived there that long. I thought he might have something in his motorhome, but there isn't enough space to put anything."

"So where else? Is there a place he went often?"

"I have no idea. At home I might be able to figure something out, but here... I never lived here and only visited him once."

"Where was that?"

"We spent most of the time at an RV park in the desert. He was still in the motorhome. We wandered around, and he showed me the Grand Canyon and a number of other spots. It was a lot of fun. We never spent more than a few days in a single place."

Knight thought for a minute. "Where did he get his mail?"

"His mail...." Day looked up and smiled. "Yes. He had the same address for the last two years. He moved around, but he had to return there every few weeks for his mail. I don't know how that helps us, but I have the address in my phone. Don't know why I kept it, but I guess I half expected him to go back on the road and return to his old ways. He was happy traveling everywhere." Day pulled up the old address. "It's just a PO box."

"That doesn't help us," Knight said and climbed out of bed, rummaging through the things on the floor. He began dressing and peered out through the curtains.

"Anything interesting out there?"

"No. We're going to be pretty screwed up for a couple of days. We've slept most of the afternoon."

"I was thinking," Day said as he got up and gathered his things together. "I'd like to see my brother's house. We didn't go in before, but I think we should now. We could contact the police and see about getting permission. It's been a couple of days, and they should have finished up by now."

"It would be ironic if he had a safe room there, given that it wouldn't be likely he could use it."

"No. But there may be something that could be a clue. Stephen has always loved puzzles, especially when we were young. He used to make treasure maps for me. That was our Easter morning. I never woke to a basket, but instead I got a piece of paper with a message that I had to decode so I could follow the trail to my basket." Day smiled. "He did things like that until I left for school. He loved making them, and if we were still living near each other, he'd probably still do it."

"Okay," Knight said skeptically. "You think he may have left some clue at the house."

"I don't know, but it's the only lead we have."

82

"All right. Let me make a few calls," Knight said, and he got on his phone.

Day finished dressing and got all their things together. He wasn't sure how long they'd be staying, but he liked things neat, and after their earlier escapades, the room was pretty disheveled.

"We'll meet you there in fifteen minutes."

"I take it we have an appointment," Day said, already heading for the door.

"Yes. The detective in charge, Royerston, is going to meet us at the house. He said he has some questions for us, and we'll have a chance to speak with him. It seems they're very interested in finding Clark Miller and don't seem to have a clue that it's a false identity."

"Maybe we should put him in touch with Simon and they can compare notes." Day was always amazed at how government agencies relished holding any information they had. Things would be a lot easier if they spoke to one another.

"True, but we can use that to our advantage if we have to." Knight tied his sneaker and joined him at the door. He took a look back, and Day knew he was committing the room to memory. Day did the same, and then they hurried out and down through the lobby to the Jeep, which was still covered in a thick layer of dirt.

"Maybe we should clean it," Day said.

Knight unlocked it and carefully got inside. "Don't touch anything you don't have to. The dirt will act as an alarm if anyone messes with the car."

Day did as instructed and settled in the seat. He knew better than to ask if Knight was being serious. He usually was in situations like this.

"Carlos Sanchez is one nasty piece of work. If we've made it onto his radar, we need to watch our backs." Knight started the engine and took off out of the parking lot, using the onboard GPS to guide them to the house.

A police car waited outside, and Day got out as the officer did the same.

"Detective Jackson Royerston."

"Dayton Ingram, and this is Knighton, a good friend," Day said, shaking the officer's hand.

"You said you're Miller's brother. Why don't you have the same last name?"

Day turned to Knight, wondering just how much they should say.

"Mr. Miller is Day's brother, but things in this case aren't necessarily as they appear."

"What the hell is that supposed to mean?" he asked, crossing his arms over his chest. "We've established that Mr. Miller wasn't at home at the time the victim was killed, and in fact, we can't establish any connection between them."

"Have you uncovered a link to Carlos Sanchez?" Knight asked.

Royerston whistled. "Shit," he swore under his breath. Apparently he hadn't. "He's involved in this?" He knitted his black brows together. "How do you know?"

"Let's go inside so we can speak privately," Knight said. "Day, get your magic equipment so we can be sure we're not overheard."

Day went back to the Jeep and retrieved a small pack from under the front seat. Then he followed the others inside and began sweeping the house.

"What the hell is he doing, and who are you guys?" Royerston was on alert, and Day thought he might draw his gun.

He let Knight do the explaining and followed a signal to listening devices in the living room and the bedroom. The kitchen seemed clear, so he motioned in there. "Someone has bugged the house," Day said quietly, and then he told the detective where the devices were.

"I repeat, who are you?" Royerston had his hands on his hips and was getting twitchier by the second.

"We work for a shadow agency, and we're here because of the disappearance of Day's brother. We weren't sure what to expect when we got here, but we didn't think we'd be messed up with something this big."

"So you don't know where Miller is either?" Detective Royerston asked.

"No," Day answered, turning to Knight as he wondered if they should give the detective the information he was missing.

"I suggest you contact Simon Craft at Border Patrol. I believe he has some information you don't have," Knight explained.

"Fuck it all. This keeps getting murkier by the second. I thought this was a straightforward domestic death, and it turns out the prime suspect wasn't here and couldn't have done it. It became obvious that the body was left here to send a message. There was little blood, and we determined she was killed somewhere in the desert. Now you're telling me Sanchez is most likely involved and is the message sender." He groaned. "We've been trying to nail that asshole for a decade. We've got plenty on him, and he operates with impunity here without ever leaving Mexico."

"Tell us about it," Day said. "All we want is to find my brother, and then we'll get out of your hair." He began looking around. "Where was the body?"

"Right over there." Royerston pointed. "Not that it told us much. Someone just dumped her."

"Is it okay if we look around?"

Royerston took a step forward. "Look, I'll agree to it as long as you promise that if you find Miller, you bring him in so we can talk to him. I'm not convinced that he doesn't know something about all this. After all, he must have pissed someone off pretty bad if they're leaving bodies in his house as a message."

Day nodded. "I'll do my best." All he wanted was to get Stephen back safe and sound. After that, there was going to be one hell of a mess to clean up. He only hoped it didn't get much bigger before that happened.

"There wasn't much in the house, as you can see. It's pretty sparse. There are a few pictures, but none of them were of you."

Day could hear the skepticism in the detective's voice. Maybe all this was bending the realm of believability for him just a little. It certainly was for Day. He thought he knew his brother well, and it turned out he knew very little about the real man.

"Maybe you should make that call to Border Patrol now, and we'll wait." Knight folded his arms over his chest and did his best not to touch a thing.

Royerston pulled out his phone and kept an eye on them. "Simon Craft, please," he said and waited. "This is Detective Jackson Royerston with Phoenix PD. I have two men who said to call you. Knighton and Ingram. ... I've had the pleasure as well. They said there was some information about Clark Miller that we might be missing. Ingram claims to be his brother. … Uh-huh. … Shit. … They checked out for you. They said that the information was yours to give. Thank you. That would be helpful." He hung up.

"Did you get what you needed?" Knight asked in that way he had that made a question sound like a command.

"Yes. It seems you two have made quite an impression on plenty of people in a short time. He told me about the alternate identity and is going to send over what he can. So your brother isn't Clark Miller, but Stephen Ingram, and this house…?"

"I don't know if it's really his or not. All I know is that he's missing and that I saw him shot on television, which was a put-up job, according to Craft, and now he's still missing."

"Jesus, what a shit show," Royerston said, and Day had to agree. "So what are you looking for?"

"Anything that might provide a clue as to where my brother is," Day explained. "All I'd like is to take a look around. We'll wear gloves so we don't contaminate your crime scene, and you can decide what you want to do about the listening devices. They might lead back to Sanchez or someone working for him."

"Okay. But if you say a word to give anything away…."

It was obvious he didn't trust them, and that was fine. Looking around was all he could ask for.

"Fifteen minutes," Detective Royerston said, and Day nodded before turning away and walking into the living room. He'd take what he could get.

He made a systematic circuit, looking at everything. The furniture and decorations were impersonal, probably from some warehouse for undercover crap. Knight followed him, questioning silently. Day shook his head and left the room, deciding to try the bedroom. That told him just as little. There were a few clothes, but nothing of a more personal nature. Day carefully checked the drawers and undersides after putting on gloves, but he found nothing at all. Everything looked as though it was a movie set. Nothing of his brother existed here.

Day pointed toward a door, and Knight followed him. He checked the bathroom and then the second bedroom, which was set up as an office.

Day stepped inside and stopped. He could see his brother in this room. Not that there were pictures of him on the walls or the desk, but the color was something Stephen would like, and the furniture had personality and weight. It wasn't crap, like the rest of the house. He motioned for Knight to look in the desk drawers and slowly walked the room. Day could almost smell his brother in here.

Knight made what looked like a bug movement on his arm. "No. This was clean," he whispered, not willing to take a chance that the others in the house were sensitive enough to pick up regular speech coming from this room.

"Anything?" Knight murmured.

"This is the only room Stephen lived in, if you know what I mean."

"It's still empty. There's very little in the drawers, and the top is clean." Knight lifted a pencil holder and placed it back on the desk. It tipped, spilling the contents onto the floor.

Day bent to gather the things up as Detective Royerston came in the room. "Wrap it up, guys. We've been through this place with a fine-tooth comb," he said softly.

"Yeah. There's nothing here," Day agreed as he picked up the holder and set it on the desk. Then he finished picking up the contents and placed them back inside, the way they had been. "We should go," he told Knight. "Thank you for everything," he said to the detective. "I know it seemed like a stupid request, but I had to try."

"Remember your promise."

"I will. But it looks like we're at a dead end, the same as everyone else." He kept his voice low and waited for the others to leave the room. Then he closed the door and walked through the house and out into the cooling early evening air. He thanked the detective for his help and took his card, promising again to call if they found anything, and then they walked out to the Jeep.

"Well, that was a complete dead end. That house was devoid of anything personal," Knight said.

"Not exactly," Day said. He reached into his pocket and pulled out the bent piece of metal that had fallen on the floor with the pens and pencils.

"What's that?"

"This was in the pencil holder, so I need to thank you for being a klutz. I never would have seen it if you hadn't knocked it onto the floor."

"What is it?"

"This is proof that Stephen did have a hiding place. When we were kids, he made things like this. They were keys to his special forts." Day grinned, twisting the black piece of bent steel in his hand.

"But if we have it, doesn't that mean he isn't using it?" Knight asked as he pulled out onto the street. He made the next turn and headed back to the hotel.

"No. He always made two keys after he lost one and spent three days trying to find it. After my parents died, Stephen let me in on his secret and showed me how he made the locks and things. He even helped me build a fort of sorts where we lived so I could have a place of my very own. That was when he told me about always making two keys. He said this type of key was pretty safe because anyone who found it would assume it was just an old piece of metal." Day stared as he turned the key between his fingers, wishing like hell it could tell him what it went to.

"So we have a key to something, but we don't know what or where."

Day closed his eyes. "I want to read the last e-mails from him again. Stephen always loved to put the pieces to his puzzles in plain sight. He had to know I wouldn't sit still and not try to help him. Maybe he was afraid the note he sent would be intercepted so he told me not to come to ensure that I would come, and if that's the case, then maybe he left other clues."

"Day, maybe you want that to be the case so badly that you're willing to turn everything on its ear to make what you want to be true."

"Do you have a better idea? If so, I'd like to hear it," Day challenged. "You can sit there and throw rocks at my ideas, but I don't hear you coming up with any yourself." He huffed and turned to watch the city outside the filthy Jeep.

"I don't have any," Knight said. "It seems like we're grasping at straws."

"Maybe, but the last one we grasped at came up with something, so what the fuck?" Day snapped and stared at Knight. He was getting a little tired of his pain-in-the-assness showing up all the damned time. "Or is it because you didn't come up with the idea?"

"That's bullshit and you know it."

"Then what is it?"

"How in the fuck should I know? We can look at the notes, or you can. There isn't anything I can do to help. I never met your brother, and I didn't grow up with him, so this brotherly code the two of you have going on isn't going to mean anything to me."

A light went on in the back of Day's head. Knight's moments of assness seemed to come out of nowhere, and Day had always thought they arose when Knight didn't want to talk about something or if Day got close to some wound. But maybe it was as simple as being needed or making a contribution. When Knight felt helpless or out of his depth, he lashed out.

"They might not, but there's plenty you can do to help."

"How?"

"Stephen loves repetition. If something was important in one of his puzzles, he repeated a word or phrase—not too much, but enough that it might hover around the edge of your brain. Making a puzzle and then not having someone solve it is no fun, so the mind leaves clues, sometimes without even meaning to. If Stephen was trying to send me some sort of message, then he'd want me to be able to understand and solve it while others can't. So he'll reuse important words multiple times, and since I'm the only one he expected to see the e-mails, then they would be things he knew would be important to me."

"Okay," Knight said.

"I'll bring up the last few e-mails he sent me before he disappeared. I don't think he'd have gone back before that. We'll look at them and see if there are any patterns. I read the messages and they seemed normal enough to me, but I wasn't looking for anything. Maybe there's nothing there after all."

"Whatever you think best. This is your show—I'm just along for the ride."

That tone was back, and Day ground his teeth.

Knight drove back to the hotel and parked the car. They got out, checked their surroundings, and then went inside. Some of the dust had blown off the Jeep so it wasn't nearly as covered, and it now just seemed extra dirty instead of like it was wearing half the desert.

Inside the hotel, they went up to their room and unlocked it. They had left the Do Not Disturb sign out. Knight held him back and opened the door, then stepped inside. "It seems okay."

Day went inside after Knight and sat at the desk, pulled his laptop from the protective case, and started it. Then he logged in to his private email and brought up Stephen's last messages. "Take a look at these and see if you see anything. At the time they seemed like Stephen's regular messages." He pulled up earlier ones and let Knight read them. Then he let Knight read the most recent ones. "Do you see anything different?" He gave Knight some time to read while he did the same, but nothing stood out.

"Not really. Is there anything in here about the puzzles or anything that might draw your attention? I keep thinking that if I were your brother and wanted to send a message, I'd send a key or something to draw your attention. The thing is, whatever it is, if it's here, it isn't going to mean anything to me." Knight turned away and paced the room.

Day returned to the e-mails. He read them again and again, but there was nothing he could see.

"Wait," Knight said. "Read this one from a few weeks ago. 'I'm looking forward to seeing you at the holidays. We can have a real Christmas like we haven't had in a long time, just the two of us. Do it right.'"

"Yeah...."

"Read the one he sent you a few days ago. 'I'm thinking we can spend Christmas the way we always have. Decide where you want to go. I was thinking the Grand Canyon would be nice, or we can find a place near Phoenix and just spend some time together.' Why did he change his mind and start talking about going somewhere?"

"I don't know. Mom and Dad used to make a huge deal over Christmas. It was Mom's favorite holiday, and she always went way out. Stephen did the best he could, but he never could do what she did. It wasn't necessary." Day sorted through some other notes. "He said he'd gotten a house for a really good price, and that he was going to be able to do some work and sell it for a lot of money." Day brought up the message. "It was from the same one where he talked about Christmas the first time." Day pointed it out.

"Did he ever send the address?"

"No. Why?"

"Look it up. If I were Clark Miller and I needed a place to hide, I'd choose something I didn't own, that was in a completely different name." Knight reached over and began looking through the open files. "Here it is. The next note. He says that the house he's working on is spectacular and that it has a pool and Jacuzzi. Maybe you could spend Christmas there. He could hide the gifts just like he used to." Knight waited. "If I were him, I'd hide there. It's not in Clark Miller's name, and I bet it would be hard for anyone to trace it. Sanchez may know he was working for someone else, but finding out his real identity might be a stretch."

"Okay. That sounds reasonable, and it isn't like Stephen to change his mind all the time, especially about something like this. So this could be a clue or it could be his situation changing."

"Yeah. But it pointed us to this other house he bought. Would there be an online record of the sale?" Knight asked.

"I don't know. Real estate records can be difficult to follow because it depends on how soon the local jurisdictions register the sale with the state. But there has to be a way to find it." Day began to think and went through the most recent e-mails again. "He said the town somewhere. The house was in the area, but not Phoenix proper. I remember something about a fountain." He began going back further and found where Stephen talked about it. "That's it, Fountain Hills."

"Then tomorrow I say we head down there and see what we can find. There are many ways to bullshit information out of people, and we may need to do that. If all else fails, we can contact the detective, but I don't want to do that unless we have to. Let's see if we can get anywhere on our own."

Day turned away from the computer. "Yeah. This could be a wild goose chase."

"Definitely, but it's all we have." Knight stepped away and handed Day the room service menu. "I'd like the chicken. Decide what you want and then call in the order. I need to clean up quick, and then maybe we can watch some television and relax. It's too late to be running around now. But we have a plan for tomorrow, and some rest is going to do us more good than worrying."

"I know. But I keep wondering about Stephen. What if all this chasing around is for nothing? What if Stephen is already dead somewhere?"

There was fire in Knight's eyes. "You have to believe that he's alive and waiting for you to find him. This defeatist attitude doesn't do anyone any good, least of all you." Knight walked closer. "In the Corps, shit happens. Lots of it. Piles of it. Shit on top of shit. We make it through because we do a job, and we tell ourselves that we're the best and that we're going to be successful. Failure is not an option. That's the attitude you have to have at times like this. Failure is not a fucking option. We'll find your brother, and he's going to be fine." Knight paused. "Don't make me slap you upside the head in order to knock this shit out of you. I will and you know it. So order dinner, and we'll eat and then get some rest."

Day did as Knight instructed, and once the food arrived, they sat down to eat. Three times during the meal, Knight got up and peered out a crack in the curtains and returned to his seat. The first time Day figured it was Knight being cautious, but after the second and then third time, he knew something was up. He set down his fork, stared at Knight, and waited.

"There's a blue Corolla sitting in front of the hotel. I think I saw it behind us when we pulled in."

"They may be staying here too," Day said, offering a simple explanation. But Knight wasn't one to push the panic button, so he perked up and his heart beat a little faster.

"True, but there's someone sitting in it. I don't know why. They can't see anything, but over the last ten minutes, I've watched the windows fog up and now they're clearing." He stepped back, rummaged in his pack, then returned with a small set of binoculars. He peered out, and Day finished the last of his food. "The window is down, and someone is definitely sitting in it."

"What do you want to do?" Day asked as he stood and walked up behind Knight. "I'm the last person to urge you not to be cautious, but why would someone sit outside our hotel?"

"What if someone else is looking for your brother too? We haven't exactly been cagey about your relationship to him. So maybe we're being followed and they're out there to see when we leave and where we go." Knight continued watching, and then he turned away and smiled.

"What?"

"A woman just raced out of the hotel and got into the car. It's gone." Knight put down the binoculars. "It was nothing."

"Maybe. But what you said makes sense. We're going to need to be careful." Day picked up the binoculars and used them to scan the parking area. "I don't see anything unusual, but we rarely do."

"Nope."

"So what should we do?"

"We'll take precautions in the morning." Knight scratched his head slowly. "Right now we need to secure things and try to get some sleep."

"Do you think we'll have visitors?"

"I don't know. But I think that if someone wanted to know where we were going, they wouldn't want us to know we were being followed. As long as we stay here and don't make a move to leave, anyone who is watching will remain that way." Knight went into the bathroom, and Day heard water running.

When Knight was done, Day cleaned up and stripped out of his clothes, then joined Knight in bed. "Can I ask you something?" Day settled close to Knight's heat and solidity. He might fight with him and enjoy pushing Knight's buttons, but Knight's strength never wavered, and neither did his loyalty. "Why don't we ever do this at home?"

"Do what?"

"Sleep in the same bed? I don't see other people, and you promised that this 'what happens on a mission, stays on a mission' thing wasn't going to continue, but it pretty much has." Day placed his hand on Knight's chest, just resting it there. "If you only want sex, and if it's just on missions to blow off steam or something, then tell me and we can deal with it. I'm getting tired of hiding. And I deserve a life that doesn't revolve around coming home from work and eating dinners for one for the rest of my life."

Knight tensed immediately. Day couldn't see his eyes, but he imagined them darkening and becoming much more intense. "We go out at home sometimes."

"But nothing changes." Day didn't press or whine. He simply stated a fact. "And if you don't want things to change, then you need to say so."

Knight didn't move, his silence broken by an eventual sigh. "I don't know what I want. I like that you're here and that I know I can count on you."

Day moved away and the bed shook a little as Knight rolled over.

"I know you're important to me and that I'd rip the head off anyone who touched you except me. I'm possessive, in case you haven't guessed."

Day scoffed. "I get that, and if anyone went for you, I'd probably knock their feet from under them with a roundhouse kick. The thing is, being jealous is nice, but what about the rest?"

Knight stroked his cheek. "Give me some time. I know I've said that before, but a lot has happened since we first met and got thrown together on that cruise. My life seemed to be going in one direction, and now it's taken a turn, and there are loads of crap that I need to wade my way through." Knight sighed one more time and then pulled him close. "I can tell you this. You, Dayton Ingram, have affected me more in some ways than anyone else I've ever met. You're exasperating and not afraid to hold a mirror up in front of me to make sure I see things as they are."

"I think I can take that." Day knew he wasn't going to get more from Knight at the moment. He'd figured out that Knight wasn't a man who spoke his feelings very often, but he showed them.

"Good. Let's try to get some sleep," Knight pronounced and shimmied closer, pressing his chest to Day's back and his hips to Day's ass.

"Are you sure sleep is what you want?" Day rolled over and climbed on top of Knight, pressing him into the mattress while he kissed him hard, taking possession of Knight's lips. Heat surged between them, and Day marveled at how quickly things always revved up between them physically. It was as if he were flame and Knight gasoline. They were combustible, and Day sometimes wondered if they wouldn't burn each other up.

Knight wound his arms around Day's waist as Day felt him surrender. That alone showed how much Knight cared.

Chapter 6

KNIGHT HAD never been comfortable talking about his feelings. That sort of thing had been trained out of him by the Corps. Weakness of any type was to be suppressed and not spoken of. That didn't mean he didn't have feelings, just that he expressed them in other ways. Like the fact that he held Day all night long, watching over him as he tossed and turned, even listening as he talked in his sleep. When Day rolled away, Knight either dozed or got up, peering out the window, trying to shake the feeling that someone was trying to bore through the walls in order to see them. The truth was, the thought of anything happening to Day made him angry and protective as hell. But he often wondered if that was because of the caring that was building inside or Marine discipline and ego. His heart had been closed off for so long, he wondered if he could trust it.

One thing he knew he could rely on was his instinct, and that was what had him sitting in the chair near the curtains, watching outside. He wanted to know if there was someone watching them. Knight knew there was equipment that could sense heat through walls or even penetrate the curtains for a microwave view inside the building. It didn't matter. Something was triggering his Marine senses, and he wasn't going to let it go. He'd relied on them too many times, and they had never failed him.

"Come back to bed," Day whispered. "Even Marines like you need to sleep."

"I'm fine." He turned to look outside once again. The feeling would not go away. "Just go to sleep. I'll come to bed in a minute." He turned back to the window. Day had rolled over, eyes closed, the bedding pressed down past his waist, just to the point where the curve of his butt was visible. *Cheryl, what should I do?* The thought that he'd ask Cheryl what he should do about her replacement made his stomach roil. God, had he gotten so maudlin that now he was listening in the dark for advice from his dead wife?

"I can hear you," Day mumbled. "All that doubt and fear running through your head." He didn't turn or move.

"Go back to sleep. You're full of shit."

"No, I'm not," Day said in the same tone. "You're sitting in that chair looking out the window and wondering about what all this means. You can tell me you're watching in case we're being watched, but you're up because you can't figure out what's going on." Day patted the bed next to him.

Knight swore to himself. What the hell *was* going on? Cheryl had had that same insight. She could always tell when he was upset about something, and she'd call him on it. "I slept too much earlier, and you need to rest so you'll be thinking clearly tomorrow." He thought about giving up and climbing back into bed, but being in closer proximity with Day would not help his ability to think.

"For an operative, you lie like shit." Day rolled over, his chest glowing in the low light. "Or maybe it's that I can tell when you're doing it."

Knight let the curtain shift back into place. He hadn't moved it much. Then he stood and got into the bed. This wasn't an argument he wanted to have at four in the morning, and fuck it, he didn't want to be talking about this shit at all. He wasn't ready to replace Cheryl with anyone, and that's what seemed to be happening. "Go to sleep."

Day shifted closer, and Knight touched him lightly to make contact. The room was a little warm, and he hoped that was what Day would think when Knight kept his distance. He needed a chance to think, and having Day pressed to him, his ass against Knight's cock, was not conducive for thinking in any way. "You too."

"Hmmm." Knight closed his eyes and cleared his mind, pushing himself to sleep, but it didn't work. He'd slept on his way to combat zones or surrounded by dozens of men chattering and talking, but this time sleep wouldn't come. There were too many voices in his head, and one of them kept saying he was being watched.

He listened, and as soon as Day's breathing evened out and he made soft sounds, just this side of a snore, Knight carefully got out of bed and took up his position once again. This time he grabbed his binoculars and scanned the parking lot below. It was well lit and seemed deserted. No one was coming or going. And if he hadn't been on alert, he might have missed the movement right out near the road. A man crossed the grass and got into a dark car parked at the edge of the lot. No light came on when he opened the door. That told Knight the man had something he was trying to hide.

He turned back to Day, watched him sleep for a few minutes, and thought about waking him. Then he decided to let him sleep. He'd keep watch for the night and think of a way to lose that man. He couldn't let anyone follow them to Fountain Hills. After searching for Day's brother, if they found him, they were not going to lead the men after Stephen to his doorstep.

KNIGHT YAWNED and went to the bathroom as the first light of dawn colored the sky. He could see the car clearly now, and there were two figures inside. He assumed they were men, and his heart rate jumped. After cleaning up, Knight pulled out his phone. "Colt, I need another favor."

"Shit, okay…. What is it?"

"We're at the Hilton Garden Inn, and we're being watched. Do you think you can get here in a few hours and meet us around by the pool in back?"

"I can do that," Colt said. "Now, do you think you could wait until it isn't the asscrack of dawn to call next time? Clarise is looking at me like I've lost my mind for taking this call."

"Tell her I'm sorry."

"See you in a few hours," Colt disconnected.

"Taking calls in the bathroom," Day teased when he came out.

"I didn't want to wake you."

"So you were on the phone, waking up someone else," Day quipped, rolling over.

"Colt is going to be here in two hours. We are being watched, so he'll pick us up out back and hopefully we can sneak out under their noses."

Day pulled up the covers. "And that couldn't wait until a decent hour of the morning? The city hall probably doesn't open until nine or ten, and it's only six. So get back in bed and shut up for a whole hour. If it will make you feel better, check that our visitors are still there and then get in here."

"I have things to do."

"Not at six in the morning. I bet even tails and human traffickers have the decency to wait until after seven before bothering people, turning on lights, making noise, and phone calls."

"Smartass," Knight said, heading to the window. The car was still there, and it looked like the two men were still in place. He let the curtain fall back and returned to the bed. The door was locked, and Knight had weapons stashed under his side of the bed. If someone did decide to make a move, he was well prepared. After pulling back the covers, he got into bed and closed his eyes. He didn't sleep, but Day seemed content, curling next to him.

"How do we know they aren't going to try something?" Day asked.

"Second thoughts?"

"Just curious."

"If they were, they would have tried early this morning, when it was unlikely anyone would be around and we would be asleep. They want something from us, but we're going to do our best to deprive them of it."

"I'm glad you have a plan," Day said with a yawn. "God, those days in the desert really took it out of me."

"It's what the desert does. Even when it's cool, it's dry enough to pull moisture out of you. You need to drink extra water because it's so dry." Knight held Day and figured he could take advantage of some quiet time. There wasn't much of that in their lives, and with the hotel being watched, they were relatively safe and he could lie here with Day for an hour before starting the day.

Knight didn't think he dozed off, but the time passed quickly. Day got out of bed and used the bathroom. Knight got up, dressed, and gathered what he thought they would need. By the time Day was dressed, he was ready to go as well.

"What about breakfast?" Day asked as Knight's phone rang.

"Don't worry about it," Knight said as he answered the phone.

"I'm ten minutes away, and I brought the necessities of life," Colt said.

"Thanks, we'll meet you around back." Knight hung up and grabbed his bag. "He's on his way. Let's head down and try not to be seen. We'll use the back stairs and hope they aren't watching out there as well."

"Didn't think of that?" Day jabbed as he hefted his bag as well.

"There's only so much I can do." He pulled out sunglasses and a ball cap from his bag. He put them on and handed some to Day. "Changes the appearance just enough that someone who isn't familiar with us won't notice who we are." Knight led the way down the hall and pulled open the stairwell door. They descended to the first floor, and Knight watched out the back door until he saw Colt's truck pull in. He signaled Day, and they walked out and got into the truck after putting the bags in the back. As soon as the doors closed, they both bent down as low as possible, and Colt pulled out.

"Are there still two men in a dark Corolla?" Knight asked as they drove around front.

"Yeah. They're watching the front and seem half asleep. Amateurs." Colt continued driving through the lot and turned out. "Where are we going?" he asked once they were away and both Knight and Day were sitting normally in their seats. "This is for you." Colt handed a cup of coffee into the back for Day and then picked the other out of the holder and handed it to Knight. "I also have donuts in the bag."

Knight passed the bag back to give Day first choice. "Fountain Hills. We think Stephen bought a house there he intended to flip, but we don't have the address. We need to get someone there to tell us which one it is."

Colt pressed on the brake and rolled his eyes before activating the Bluetooth. "Clarise, the guys need info about a house in Fountain Hills that Day's brother bought."

"Stephen Ingram," Day supplied.

"I can only get what's public record," Clarise said.

"All they need is the address," Colt said.

"Give me a minute," she said, and they waited while cars went past them. "Okay, it's 1987 Prospect."

"Thank you so much," Day said from the back, and Colt thanked her as well before disconnecting. "It helps to have a wife who sells real estate and knows everyone." Colt put the address in his GPS and then pulled back into traffic, speeding up as they followed the mechanical-sounding female voice to the address.

Both Day and Colt whistled when they pulled up in front of the huge, immaculate house.

Knight turned to Day and then got out of the truck once Colt parked in the drive. It was best if they looked as though they belonged there. "Where do we go?" Knight asked in a quiet tone.

"Stephen said we were to go in back and wait for him there," Day answered loud enough that anyone who might overhear would think they were normal visitors.

The backyard was fenced, but after Knight did a little jimmying, the gate opened easily, and they walked in back. The swimming pool sparkled in the bright sun, inviting and fresh, the concrete around it newly cleaned, while the landscaping was still rough, with some areas dug up and others still filled with weeds. Some areas had been left to die.

"Okay, where should we start?" Knight asked quietly. "If your brother were to hide something here, where would he do it?" He pulled off his sunglasses. "You said he was planning to sell the house eventually, so he couldn't have built something into the house itself."

"I agree. It has to be something hidden, yet accessible. Like I said, Stephen liked puzzles and riddles." Day walked to the back door and peered into the house, and Knight did the same. Some drop cloths and cans of paint sat near one of the walls. The kitchen itself was impressive: stainless-steel appliances, granite surfaces, shimmering tile backsplash. "He said he got really lucky when buying this house, but, man...."

"This is an awesome neighborhood, and once the house is done, it'll sell for a lot," Colt said. "But that doesn't get us any closer to why we came here."

"No." Day turned away and began looking through the yard. "To tell you the truth, I was hoping I'd find him here."

"No. That would be too easy a trail for someone to follow. Border Patrol would certainly have looked here for him, and what was he going to do, bury himself under the foundation?"

"No," Day said and walked closer to the house. "When we were kids, we lived in an older house, and there was a cistern in one corner of the basement. It was no longer in use, and you could get to it through a trapdoor in the kitchen floor. I remember him going down into it when Mom and Dad were gone—scared the crap out of me—and he said he found where one wall had been opened up. It was dry and there were cupboards in Mom's laundry room in front of it. Stephen cut through the back of the cupboards to get to the opening. The cistern became a hideout for us. Drove Mom and Dad crazy, because he'd just disappear. Finally they made him tell them where he went." Day smiled. "I remember Mom being really mad and Dad smiling. Now I know he was proud of him."

"What does that have to do with here?" Colt asked. "There aren't basements or cisterns here, not really. Most houses are built on concrete pilings and slabs."

Day nodded and walked the edge of the house. "He could have tunneled beside the slab to put something in."

Colt shook his head. "It would weaken the slab."

"What about the pool house?" Knight asked.

"It's nice enough, but little more than a fancy shed," Colt said, but Day made his way over and went inside.

"It's definitely more than a shed. There's a changing room and bathroom," Day said as he came back out. "No extra space at all." He continued exploring the area around the pool. "We should go. I don't want to break into the house and find there's nothing here." He sounded defeated. "I don't have any choice but to wait to see if Stephen decides to call me. If he's in hiding, then he's determined to stay there for some reason." He walked toward the gate, then stopped and knelt down next to a concrete dog statue.

"What is it?" Knight asked.

"Where did that come from?" Day examined it closer. "This was my mother's. She had it in one of her flower beds when we were growing up, and we kept it in the yard after she died. Stephen must have kept it."

"Is there anything else here that's part of your past?"

"No. It's only a house that Stephen is fixing up to sell."

"Then why is it here?" Knight asked, bending his knees and then lifting the dog onto the sidewalk. The bed had been recently mulched, and the dog sat on top of it. Knight kicked the light shredded plastic mulch to the side and his foot scraped something hard.

Day leaned in and cleared away an unpainted, brushed metal surface about a foot square.

"This is homemade," Colt said.

Knight brushed the lid with his hand and moved a cover that concealed a small hole.

Day smiled and pulled out the piece of metal they'd found at the house the day before. He inserted it and turned. A small click sounded, and Day pulled, lifting the lid.

"What's inside?" Knight asked.

Day hesitated, then reached inside and drew out a notebook. He sat back and opened the pages.

Knight wasn't ashamed to peer over his shoulder. The writing wasn't in a language he could read. He looked in the bottom of the container. It was lined with money—a lot of money. He couldn't help but wonder if that was the source of the trouble that had started this. Had Stephen been undercover but decided the money he was seeing was too much of a temptation and decided to start a retirement fund? Knight kept quiet, for now, only because he knew it would upset Day.

"Can you read it?" he asked as Day leafed through the pages.

"He's writing in French. That was Stephen's foreign language of choice in school. He was very good at it, and I'm thinking he didn't expect to encounter many French speakers here." Day turned the page. "This is a schedule." His eyes widened and he looked around. "Holy shit." He put the book back, but then reached for it again. "I need a pen."

Colt pulled one out of his pocket.

Day thumbed to the back of the book, ripped out a page, and wrote. *You need to call me right away. —Day.* He folded the page and set the book and note back in the box, closed the lid, and then respread the mulch. "Put the dog back exactly as you found it. We need to get the hell out of here."

"Okay," Knight agreed, seeing the instant tension lines around Day's mouth.

"Stephen was supposed to be here, but he must have forgotten. I called and left him a message. We might as well go and try to see him later," Day said out loud, which Knight assumed was for the benefit of anyone listening. Day opened the gate and led the way down the drive to Colt's truck and got in the back before turning toward them, his expression asking why they were taking so long.

"What was all that about?" Knight turned to ask once he and Colt were inside and the doors closed.

"Please, just drive."

Knight blinked a few times and shifted his gaze to Colt and then back to Day. Knight was getting angry and about to lash out, but the set of Day's jaw told him to hold his tongue.

"Where to?"

"Anywhere safe and away from any prying ears or eyes." He'd gone paler than usual, which told Knight there was something wrong. "Fucking hell."

Colt backed down the drive and onto the road, going a moderate speed. "I saw that car pass the house," he said as an old Oldsmobile passed them going the other way.

"Speed up and either lose them or make them declare themselves," Knight said.

Colt sped up, taking the first corner and then another, nearly running a light at the entrance to the subdivision. Horns sounded after them.

Knight turned and saw the Olds make the turn a ways behind them.

Colt sped as fast as he dared, weaving in and out of traffic, putting as many cars between them as possible. "I wanted some of the old excitement," Colt said with a smile, making another turn and then yet one more, sliding into a quiet street and then turning once more to come onto another street. The GPS voice, which Colt had set to take them back to the hotel, seemed to be going nuts with the constantly changing directions. It would have been funny if they weren't being tailed so closely.

"Get down," Knight called when he saw a glint from a passing car. He thought they'd lost them. Everyone ducked, and Colt's rear driver's side window shattered. Knight couldn't return fire, but Day did, and the car fell back, careening into a light pole.

"Blowouts are a bitch," Day said as he put the gun beside him on the seat. "That's one hell of a weapon you got, Colt."

"Thanks. Now don't blame me if I want to get the hell out of here and away from you two as fast as I can. I've been shot at plenty enough to last a lifetime."

"Sorry about the window," Knight said.

"You'll get it paid for, right?"

"Of course," Knight said as Colt drove as fast as possible without having every cop in Phoenix on their tail. "Drop us at a rental car agency. We've put you in enough danger and don't need to add to it."

"What about the Jeep?"

"We'll have them pick it up. That should confuse who's been watching us. Our important stuff is in back of your truck, and we'll figure out how to get the rest from the hotel. You also might want to put your truck in the garage and get Clarise to a hotel for a few days. Call the police. Say you were shot at on the road. Make as big a deal of it as possible. They don't want to call attention to themselves any more than they can help. Hopefully as long as they aren't mentioned, they'll back off you and go back to looking for us."

"This is really messed up," Colt commented. "What was in that box?" he demanded, turning to Day.

"You don't want to know," Day answered, and Knight wondered what could be so explosive. But he obviously didn't want to talk in front of Colt.

Colt took them to a rental car agency downtown and dropped them off.

They grabbed their bags from the back. Knight handed Colt some extra cash from his bag. "Disappear for a few days—stay out of sight and make a big show of leaving, so the neighbors know you're going away."

"What if they follow us or show up?"

"Give them our names and say how pissed you are that your truck got shot. You blame us and don't care if you ever see us again. Say we're leaving to go back to Milwaukee, and good riddance."

Colt nodded. "This was amazing."

Knight sighed. "Just stay cautious and get out of town. I'm sorry I got you involved in this."

"Yeah, me too," Day agreed, and they watched as Colt pulled away before carrying their bags into Hertz.

They gave Day a hard time because he didn't have a reservation, but eventually rented him a Mazda, and then they were out of there and back on the road.

"What was in the box?" Knight asked as soon as they got underway.

"The book was some notes Stephen took. It contained a schedule for one of Sanchez's upcoming trips. It seems there are a lot of problems in Albuquerque, and he's planning to go there next week to take care of them. Sounded like the problems were ones Stephen was able to cause, and now Sanchez has to sort them out personally."

"So he's going to be in the US, personally."

"Yeah."

Knight whistled. "It might not happen, after what's gone down."

"Don't know. But now I partially understand why Stephen's in deep hiding. He wants to seem dead so this trip will play out."

"Do you really think Sanchez bought the act?" Knight asked.

Day nodded. "Stephen was angry at the man who shot him. So I think Sanchez must think Stephen was indeed shot. But I bet he's figured out that Stephen was undercover, and now they're trying to figure out what he knew and who he told."

"So we're on his radar screen," Knight mumbled and then swore under his breath. They were just two guys against the organization that Sanchez could bring to bear. This was not good. "What the hell are we going to do?"

"I don't know. You saw that I left a message in the box, and I'm hoping that when Stephen retrieves what he's hidden, he'll be shaken up enough that he'll actually make contact. But I don't know. There are so many things about this whole fucking situation that make me angry."

Knight mulled possibilities in his mind. They had been in situations like this before. "We need to find a place where we can hole up for a while and wait to see if he contacts us. What do you think about telling Simon what we found? We need some local support. Dimato is hours away." The information about Sanchez had gripped him with both excitement and the same fear he saw in Day's eyes.

"I don't know." Day hesitated as he watched the road. "If Stephen hasn't told them, then I'm not going to. There has to be a reason, and I have to trust him. This is really his show, and we came up on the scene because he disappeared and I wasn't going to sit by and wait." Day turned and began heading toward the south end of town. "There was a cluster of hotels that we passed before hitting the desert with Colt. We're going there, where there's plenty of people coming and going."

"Good. What about the rest of our stuff?"

Day turned to him and smiled. "I thought about that. Everything is packed up. Call the hotel and tell them that we've had an emergency. Ask if they'll finalize the bill and put our bags in storage for a few days. We can pick them up later."

Knight made the call, and the hotel agreed to help them. Of course, he couldn't ask if the car with the guys who'd been watching them was still there. God, this whole thing was too much. "Maybe I'm getting too old for this," Knight said with a shudder.

"Maybe we both are. I wanted field work so badly, and now we've both been shot and we're on the run from God knows who, looking for my missing brother. We were shot at again today." Day shook his head. "Sometimes a desk job looks pretty damn good." He gripped the wheel hard enough that his knuckles turned white. "I hope like hell this works, and we can be safe for a little while."

"I keep wondering why they're following us," Knight said.

Day snorted.

"I know we crossed paths in the desert, but we didn't interfere with their business, and they were going to have to choose a new route regardless, after the shooting and all. We've been looking for Stephen, not poking into Sanchez's operation." He sat back, letting his mind wander. "My thoughts keep coming back to a leak somewhere."

"Maybe that's why Stephen is hiding. He doesn't know who to trust with the information he has," Day suggested.

"It's a good theory, but one we aren't going to get answers to until Stephen surfaces." Knight was running hot and fast. He could feel each of his senses, heightened and on alert. He watched every car in front of or behind them. They all behaved normally, and for now he was pretty sure no one was following them.

"So we do what I couldn't when we were at home. We sit and wait." Day groaned. "Maybe we'd all have been better off if I'd have done that in the first place." He continued driving and pulled into a Comfort Inn.

The parking lot was fairly empty, and Knight got out to see if they had rooms available. After paying with his credit card and filling out the registration, they had a room. He told Day where to park the car so they could keep an eye on it based on where their room was located, and they got their bags and climbed to the second floor.

Knight unlocked the room door, and they went inside. "We contact no one for now. The car is fairly untraceable, and we're at a different hotel. We lay low and wait for Stephen to call."

"What about food? This hotel isn't going to have room service."

"Just act like any other tourists, and no one is going to pay us any attention." Knight set down his bag and sank into the single chair in the corner. "For now we do nothing and say nothing. Let them think we've dropped off the face of the earth. If we aren't interfering with their business, they'll move on to something else."

"I hope you're right."

Day was never the best at waiting... for anything. It made him a good operative, but sometimes things required patience. Knight was good at that and usually used those times for sleep and quiet. But at the moment, he was way too keyed up, and after about ten seconds, he stood and walked over to Day, then pushed him down on the bed.

"What's this?"

"Call it stress relief, call it tension, call it needing to fuck you through the mattress." Knight pressed his lips to Day's, and instantly the energy he was giving out came back tenfold. Day was a live wire, and Knight was afraid he was going to get electrocuted, but then he always was a risk-taker.

Knight paused and blinked as that thought flashed through his mind. He looked down into Day's blue eyes, roiling with too many emotions and contradictions to count.

"I'm tempted to kick your ass to the floor," Day told him roughly.

"Why?"

"You want to fuck when you want to fuck, but when it comes to what's important, you back away." Day placed his hands on his cheeks. "You need to figure out what the hell you really want. I'm not just some guy you fuck when you want to and then keep waiting while you make up your mind about whatever is going through that narrow, minute Marine brain of yours."

"Minute?" Knight asked, a smile breaking out despite how much he wanted to be angry.

"Sometimes you have such a peabrain. There are other people in this world besides you and your needs."

Knight lifted himself off Day and stood, wondering where this was coming from. "What the hell?"

"What the fuck do you mean? You're all keyed up and want to use sex to blow off some steam. I'm all for that if that's all this is." Day stood too, staring at him, daring Knight to argue. "You've been lost in your own world of grief and self-pity. I know you cared about Cheryl and Zachary, and that they were taken from you, but I'm not your sex toy. I have needs of my own, and you seem to slough them off as though they aren't important."

"I never said that," Knight said, blinking as he wondered where this came from all of a sudden.

"My family is gone. Stephen was all I had… have… and I can't find him. We think he's in hiding, but what if he's not? What if he's dead? Should I just lie back on the fucking bed, looking up at you while you get your jollies, and pretend that everything is fine because Orville Knighton got what he wanted and that's all that matters?" Day stepped closer, jabbing him in the chest with his finger. "Maybe I want more than the pittance you're willing to give me. All this seems to be bringing a lot of the shit in my life into focus. If Stephen is gone, it will rip my heart out, but I'll find a way to go on with my life, and I'll build a family of my own, somehow."

"Day, I… I…." Knight stuttered.

"What? You expect me to just wait while you think about what you want? Sometimes I wonder if I'll grow old and gray while you work through whatever shit you can't seem to get past."

"My wife and child were taken away from me. Killed," Knight blazed, without raising his voice, but Day stepped back at the intensity.

"And it's possible my brother was too. So just like you, I may have lost the person most important to me. And is it too much to ask that maybe I'd want some comfort or someone to say 'Hey, it's going to be all right, and we'll get through this, whatever happens'? Rather than 'I want to fuck you through the mattress'? I know I'm a guy, and in your world, a guy will fuck anything anytime, day or night, doesn't matter. The world comes to an end, let's fuck. Your brother may have been killed, let's fuck. Well, maybe I don't want to."

"Okay. All you had to do was say so," Knight said.

Day shook his head. "You know something? If it's possible, I think your brain is getting smaller by the minute. Just go over there and do something. Hell, go in the bathroom and jerk off if that's what you need to do. Bust a nut, and when you feel more human, then maybe you can come out and have a conversation that doesn't revolve around your dick." Day shook and turned away, stomped to the chair in the corner, and flopped into it. He glared back at Knight and then looked out the windows toward the desert.

Knight was so confused, he had no idea what to say. He ended up going into the bathroom, closing the door harder than necessary, and staring into the mirror. He hadn't thought he'd done anything wrong. He and Day were fucking. He'd never asked for a forever kind of thing, and they'd never made any promises to each other. "Shit…," Knight groaned. How could Day expect him to let go of Cheryl like that and just replace her? There was no way he could do that. Things between them were complicated, and he realized now that she deserved so much better than him. "What should I do?" Of course, he didn't get an answer from his reflection. This wasn't *Snow White*, and hell, he certainly wasn't Prince Charming.

Knight splashed water on his face and dried it with a towel, then opened the door and walked back into the room. Day hadn't moved. "Maybe you're right," Knight said.

"About what?" Day asked without turning to look at him.

"I don't have the faintest clue."

Day turned away from the window, rolling his eyes. "I daresay that's the most insightful thing I think I've ever heard you say. Not that I have a clue about shit either." He turned back to what seemed fascinating outside.

Knight sat on the edge of the bed, watching Day.

"You know, it's funny," Day finally said after a silence that seemed interminable settled over the room.

"What is?"

"I haven't the faintest clue about things either. I haven't had a relationship with a guy before, and neither have you. I guess I thought there wouldn't be this teenage angst and all this emotional shit. I figured I'd meet a guy, we'd fuck, have great sex that would blow his mind… and we'd figure out that we were good together and we'd go through the rest of our lives having great sex and being the envy of everyone we knew."

"That's pretty naïve," Knight said.

"Yeah, so sue me. I had no idea that caring for someone would be like knocking my head against a brick wall on a constant basis." Once again he didn't look at Knight. Maybe it was easier for him to say what he had to without eye contact.

For Knight it was frustrating as hell.

"Look at me. If you want to stay away, then say so, but have the decency to look at me. I'm not the person behind the counter at the drugstore."

"And that's the problem. You're someone I can count on. You've held my life in your hands just like I've safeguarded yours. Other than Stephen, you know me better than anyone else in the world, and I'm not interesting enough for you to bother with, other than to fuck."

"I never said that. I need time."

"Knight," Day snapped. "You've had years. I know you were in the bag for most of it, but didn't you ever think about what you had and grieve? Were you in complete pickled suspended animation during that time, or did you simply decide that you didn't want to feel or deal with any of it and then maybe the tragedy hadn't happened?"

"How do I just let them go?" Knight asked.

"Is that what you've been trying to do? Because you don't. They'll be part of you, just like my parents are part of me. They're gone, but I carry them with me always. Stephen raised me, but he didn't take their place, and no one is going to take Cheryl and Zachary's place."

"It doesn't feel that way." This was so strange for him. He rarely talked about his feelings. Yet with Day he could talk about anything and knew it would be treated with respect and care. That was Day's real gift. "The pain is still there, just like they had died yesterday."

"That's bullshit," Day challenged, turning to glare at him. "Now you're using them as an excuse or a wall to hide behind. And yes, Marines can hide. I know you won't admit it, but you're scared. Everyone you care about isn't going to be taken from you."

Knight wasn't so sure about that. He'd lost plenty and spent enough time alone to think that maybe that was his natural state. "Maybe I'm meant to be alone."

"That's cop-out number two," Day said. "You want to go for three?" He cocked his eyebrows and waited.

Knight clamped his lips together, figuring it didn't matter what he said at this point.

"What do you really want, Knight?"

He looked at Day, his gaze traveling over his full lips, magnificent eyes, and down his muscled chest, slim hips, and strong legs. He'd seen him in action, running like the wind, fast, determined, as capable as any Marine he'd ever fought with. He knew exactly what he wanted, but guilt and fear kept building a wall he couldn't seem to get over or around. He had told Day about fear and how he needed to use it, but he hadn't explained that there were different kinds of fear. He could deal with the usual kind—people shooting at him, the sounds and feel of battle—but this thing with Day wasn't a battle. It was something else, with bigger stakes that he wished he could put a name to. He didn't have one, only the deep-seated knowledge that if he let Day truly into his heart, then something else would have to go.

Knight lay back on the bed, staring at the ceiling, trying to figure things out. How could he tell Day that he wanted both? He wanted the pain and hurt of loss to fade and the excitement and unabashed passion that Day brought in his life, but if he embraced the one, the other would slip away. They were his family, and his memories were all he had left of them. If the hurt that still resided inside diminished, then he'd lose part of them.

He pulled out his wallet, peering over at Day, who was staring out the window. Knight opened the wallet slowly and drew out the picture he kept inside. Cheryl and Zachary smiled out from the image, eyes bright. Zachary had looked just like his mother. He had her eyes and smile. Knight kept the picture with him but didn't look at it much.

"When is that from?" Day asked.

Knight swore inwardly because he hadn't heard him approach. "I took it just before my last mission. We were in the backyard. You can see the flowers Cheryl planted behind them. She had a green thumb and could make anything grow, and he…. I was so proud of him. He was my son, the only one I'm ever going to have." Fucking hell, he was not going to shed more tears over them. He'd done that enough already, but he felt the tightness in his throat and was tempted to punch Day in the face to start a fight, something to overshadow the maudlin feelings that threatened to take over.

"Don't you dare," Day said. "I can see that battle look in your eyes. It's time you dealt with this rather than covering it up with alcohol or testosterone."

"How did you know? And what do you think you're going to do about it?"

Day leaned closer. "We've already fought once, and I cleaned your clock—never forget that. The second time, I'll make sure you never have children again, and every time you try to get it up, Mr. Happy will turn a little shy. Am I making myself clear?" He cocked an eyebrow.

"Shit…," Knight said.

"So tell me something else about them."

"Zachary loved to draw. He was really good. Cheryl kept a box of his drawings. I have it in the top of my closet. And in the spring, the two of them used to plant so many flowers in the yard that it looked like a florist shop. I remember Cheryl doing all her planting one year when Zachary was about five, I think. She came in to show me what she'd done, and when we came out, there was Zachary, going from plant to plant, picking each and every flower, his little hands filled with them. 'Look, Mommy, I picked you flowers,' he said to her, looking up with a smile."

Day nodded.

"Neither of us had the heart to scold him, but Cheryl did stop him from picking more flowers, and, of course, in a week or so, more flowers grew and everything was okay. But that entire summer, we had to caution him to ask before he picked the flowers or our entire garden would have ended up in vases." Knight closed his eyes.

"You know those memories will always be with you. It isn't like moving on will wipe them away. Instead, you'll make new ones."

Knight sat up. "There are some days when I have to try hard to remember his face or his smile and Cheryl's laugh. I tried to remember what she sounded like and couldn't. I still can't. It may seem stupid, but if I replace them, then their memories will continue to fade. They died because of me. You know more about what happened than you should."

"Not nearly enough to help."

"You can't. I did what I had to in Panama, and it cost me my family. Colt and the other men lived, but now we know that the price for their lives was the life of my wife and son."

Day sat on the bed and then slowly lay down next to him. "If you had it to do over, would you change anything? Would you hesitate and not do whatever it was that saved the others?"

Knight had asked himself that same question more times in the last few weeks than he could count, but he'd never been able to answer it. Each outcome was pretty awful. He stared at the ceiling, blinking, trying to be honest.

"There isn't a wrong answer," Day whispered.

"Maybe," Knight said, and Day slid his hand into his.

"We make the decisions that are best at the time," Day said. "Panama happened years before Cheryl and Zachary were killed. You had no way of knowing what the consequences of doing your duty and standing up for brotherhood were going to be." Day squeezed his hand tighter. "Would you do anything different?"

"No," Knight answered as water began welling up behind the dam inside him, cresting, pushing, and then rolled over it to crash down the other side. He reached up and wiped his wet cheek. He closed his eyes again, but tears still came rolling down.

Day held his hand harder, practically squeezing his fingers until they hurt, and Knight held him back, knowing he was moments from falling apart completely.

Chapter 7

DAY SAT with Knight, saying nothing, feeling him falling to pieces. He'd been giving Knight grief—a lot of it—for being distant, and in a few seconds, that distance had evaporated. Day fully understood that Knight was a man of action and that emotions weren't his forte. Talking about them was even more foreign, but the fact that he trusted Day enough to let go of some of the pent-up grief for his wife and son in front of him was heart-wrenching and warming in a strange, backhanded way. Knight was the kind of man who'd dig himself a hole, hide, and fall to pieces alone, emerging when the tide that had washed over him had passed on and he'd had a chance to dry out so no one would know what had happened.

"I'm going to get us something to eat," Day said softly. He figured they could both use food, and Knight could use the privacy. "I'll walk nearby and get us something."

Knight lay still, his arm draped over his eyes.

Day grabbed one of the room keys and left, making sure the door closed behind him. Then he jogged down the hall and stairs before exiting by a side door.

In the dry sunshine, he looked into cars, checking for guys sitting or hanging around. He saw nothing and walked across the parking lot. There were a number of fast-food restaurants nearby, judging by the signs, and he headed for a fried chicken place. He crossed the road and went inside.

There was a short line, and when his turn came, he ordered and stood aside to wait. He scanned the restaurant and thankfully saw no one he recognized. His number was called, and he picked up his food, thanked the man, and headed for the door. Then he stopped, turned around, and quickly strode across the restaurant and out the doors on the other side. Swearing under his breath, he walked around the building, keeping low and ducking between cars. He reached the edge of the parking lot, ducked across the strip of land to the street, and hurried across as soon as it was clear.

He turned on the other side, checked that the coast was clear, and walked to the hotel as fast as he could without running to bring attention to himself. He scanned his key, and as soon as the door closed behind him, he raced up to their room and let the door slam once he was inside.

"Javier, the guy from the desert, came into the restaurant as I was leaving." Day gasped for breath and set the food on the table. "I don't think he saw me, but that's the last thing we need."

"You forgot your phone," Knight said as he handed it to him.

Of course, there were no calls, and Day set out the food. Knight was feeling better, judging by the relaxed expression on his face, which relieved Day. At least he'd schooled his expression. "Aren't you concerned?"

"About Javier? No. I'm sure you made sure he didn't see you, and there isn't any way that anyone can know we're here. We weren't followed, and we paid with cash under an identity that we've never used here in town. It's just a coincidence, and we have enough to be concerned with at the moment." Knight came over and sat down.

"I don't get you, and I suppose I never will."

"Nope. Mystery is what keeps life interesting," Knight quipped.

"Then ours is interesting all the way to the moon right now," Day said. "We have plenty of it."

"Maybe not as much as you think. I'm pretty convinced your brother is alive and out there somewhere. Why he hasn't done anything with the information he has is a bit of a mystery still, but I'm sure he has his reasons. I think one of the things we need to figure out is what we're going to do about Sanchez. We're on his radar now, and we are going to need to get off it. This guy has power and a lot of reach. I'm not sure how far that reach extends, but I don't want to push it."

Day nodded. "We have to wait and see if Stephen comes forward. If he is alive, then his plans determine what we do." He hated that his pessimism crept into his remark, but he couldn't help it. The last he'd seen of his brother was him being shot, and he couldn't let that go. It didn't matter if it was a put-up job or if they hadn't found blood at the scene. It still kept playing in his mind, over and over again.

"We'll give it two days. After that, we have to assume that Stephen isn't going to contact you, and we'll have used up most of the time Dimato gave us."

Day picked up a piece of chicken, holding it halfway to his mouth. "I'm not leaving here without knowing. I can't go back and wonder what's going on with my brother. If we don't hear anything, then you can go back. I'll move into Stephen's motor home if I have to. But leaving Stephen dangling in the wind isn't an option."

"What about your job? You've fought hard for what you wanted." Knight picked up a thigh, but didn't take a bite, staring at him over the piece of chicken.

"It's a job. Stephen is family. If something happened to your family, wouldn't you do the same?" Day knew things between Knight and his ultraconservative family were rough, but they were still his family.

Knight hesitated. "I don't fucking know." He set down the food and sat back. "I'm not hungry anymore."

Day was surprised. "Thinking about your family gets under that Marine exterior and makes you lose your appetite?" That was shocking.

"If you grew up the way I did…. No, I actually don't know if I'd lift a finger to help them." Knight paused a few moments, and Day took a bite, chewing absently, not really tasting the food, his attention on Knight. "They rejected me when I decided to become a Marine and they… well, he… my father… never accepted Cheryl or Zachary." Knight picked up his chicken and tore into it like a starving dog, with a lot more intensity than was necessary. "I took them to visit after Zachary was born, and he refused to hold his grandson. When Cheryl offered the baby to him, he said he had to work on his sermon and left the fucking room. I will never forget the look on her face as long as I live. The light that Cheryl always had in her eyes, that sparkle, went out as though he'd thrown an ocean of water on her."

"Jesus. What did you do?"

"I was taught respect as a child. My father was all about respect. As a Marine, I learned that there's respect for the rank, and respect for the man in the rank. Respect for rank is built into military discipline and following orders, but respect for the man is earned. I'll never forget marching down the hallway, opening the door to my father's office,

116

stepping inside, and slamming the door so hard it nearly went off the wall. My father jumped half a foot. 'You don't do that here,' he said."

Day stopped eating for a moment.

"'I will do as I wish, Old Man,' I told him. 'I'm not a child, and you will respect me and my family. I don't care about your feelings or your petty need for control. Cheryl is my wife and Zachary is my son. And don't think for a minute that I don't know what this is about: control and your pride. You can say whatever you want, but according to the crap you've been preaching for years, you're well on your way to hell. So be afraid.' I turned, yanked open the door, and stormed out, then gathered Cheryl and lifted Zachary from my mother's arms. We hadn't been there an hour, and our things were still in the car. I gently escorted Cheryl out of the house, and we strapped Zachary into his car seat and went home."

Day couldn't fathom a family like that and wasn't sure what to say. It explained a great deal about the hurt and pain that seemed to reside so deep inside Knight.

"I spoke to my mother every once in a while, when she could call. Mom was always afraid my father would find out, and she wouldn't go against him. The only time I called was to tell my parents that Cheryl and Zachary had been killed. My father told me it was God's will or some such pile of shit. I hung up on the bastard and haven't spoken to him since. So you ask if I'd help them… I don't know. They haven't done anything for me."

Day ate slowly. "Yeah, but having a fight is one thing. What if they needed you?" He took a bite of the chicken leg and set the bone down. "What if your dad or mother, even one of your brothers or sisters, was in real trouble…?" He stared at Knight. In the back of his mind, he knew this was a test of trust and faith. "Would you put that aside and go help?"

Knight dropped what was left of his piece of chicken on the black plastic plate. "I know the answer you want. And I wish I could give it to you. But the truth is, I just don't know. I'm not really a part of my family any longer. I suppose if my mom needed me enough to call and say that she wanted my help, I'd go. But my dad…."

Day nodded. "That's an honest answer." His phone chimed and Day snapped it up, the air instantly whisking from his lungs. He stared at the screen and then showed it to Knight.

"Stephen?" Knight asked.

The number was strange, but Day nodded. All it said was *Dayton?*

He answered and waited, the food forgotten as his heartbeat increased tenfold in a second.

We need to meet.

Where and when? Day sent and waited once again.

He sent an address. *Is Knight with you?*

Yes. He's coming. Don't argue, Day sent, and he could almost hear his brother sigh in his mind.

Three was the reply, and that was all.

Day sent *Okay* and waited for more but heard nothing. "We have a place and time," Day muttered.

"Yeah. But we don't know if it's him. All you got were texts from a strange phone."

"No," Day corrected, "he knew about you by name. Stephen would know that, and I doubt others would. Stephen and I have talked about it, and he understands how things are between us. I think that was his way of saying that it was really him, but your caution is probably for the best. We'll arrive early to have a look around, make sure it's him." Day could hardly contain his excitement and relief. It seemed Stephen was truly all right, and as he put down the phone, the tension and worry he'd been carrying started to fall away.

"It's going to be okay," Knight said, and Day wondered why he'd said it. Then he realized he'd been sitting still, staring without seeing anything. "Go ahead and finish eating. We've been keeping weird hours, to say the least, and whatever happens, we're going to need to be on our toes." Knight lowered his gaze and returned to his lunch.

Day figured he was right and did the same.

HE SPENT much of the intervening hours trying not to pace the hotel room. Knight went out and returned an hour later dressed like some demented cowboy in strange clothes, but carrying their things from the old hotel. "Apparently they're still watching the place. I was able to get in and out without Tweedledee and Tweedledum in the car realizing it. I can't figure out why they haven't moved on."

"Maybe they're covering all their bases or those guys were there to watch someone else," Day said, and Knight rolled his eyes.

"So Phoenix is now the stakeout capital of the country, with everyone watching everybody else?"

"Who the hell knows? They followed us to my brother's somehow, so unless they're complete idiots—and that's always a possibility—they have to know we aren't there."

"There's another possibility, and one that's scarier. What if more than one person is after your brother? It's a lot easier to stay out of the way of one person, but what about two? Being caught in the crossfire is enough to scare the shit out of just about anyone. I've seen brave men fall to the ground, gripping the dirt, praying like hell when that happens, because it's about the only thing you can do."

"Okay. So what do we do to help?"

Knight stood and walked right in front of him, staring hard enough to freeze water in an instant. "We listen to him, and then do what he wants."

"Knight...."

"I know you. You say I'm an ass, but you're as stubborn as one. Hell, there are times when you out-stubborn me, and that's saying something. When you think you're right, you'll stand your ground no matter what anybody tells you. But this is one time you have to listen to Stephen and do what he asks. If he wants our help, we'll give it, without question. But if he asks us to go home, we'll be on the next plane back."

"You don't even know what he has to say."

"No, I don't. But we've stuck our noses into something a lot bigger than either of us realized, and it may have made things worse. You know it, and so do I. We don't fuck with our brothers, and we always have their backs, and sometimes that means we have to let them make their own choices and walk away. That's the hardest part of brotherhood. We're there when they need us, and willing to say good-bye and trust that they know best when they don't." Knight's voice faltered, and he pulled out a chair before falling into it.

"What?" Day asked, seeing the dark pall that settled in Knight's eyes.

"I was on my first tour in Iraq. A cocky kid just out of training, with all that Marine pride and bravado bursting out of me. We got into our first firefight, and three of us were separated from our unit. We were alone, at night, in the middle of the desert. Scary as hell. I heard the enemy and raised my gun, ready to shoot. Jones, he shook his head, said to sit tight, hide. I was so itchy, I overruled him and shot. Killed the enemy where he stood. Didn't count on a second man, who took out Jones before Skeeter could get him." Knight swallowed. "Sometimes you have to walk away from a fight."

"So you're saying…."

Knight leaned closer. "Don't be purposely dense. If your brother asks us to walk away, we will. Without hesitation. You have to trust that he knows what's best, even if it isn't what you want."

"What if I do and something happens to him?" Day asked.

"Then it was his choice, and you'll be able to live with that. Let me ask you this: What if you don't and something happens to him? Can you live with that?" Knight cocked his eyebrow. "I had to learn to live with what happened years ago, and it wasn't easy. You don't want to find yourself in that position." Knight checked his watch. "We should get going soon if we want to be there early and scope things out."

"All right."

"To what?" Knight pressed.

"We'll go and I'll do what he asks me to do." Day hated the thought of walking away from Stephen, but he'd do it if he had to.

He hoped Stephen didn't ask.

LESS THAN an hour later, they pulled up to what looked like a warehouse. The building had seen better days, and the once red-painted walls were sandblasted either pink or paintless by the desert. Shipping containers lay on the ground around it.

Day got out and stood near the gate, peering between the chain-link to see if anyone was around inside. He saw no movement and turned back to where Knight sat looking at him.

"If he's here, he'll show himself when he's ready," Knight said.

Day got back in the car, and Knight rolled down the windows, and turned off the engine. "What are we going to do?"

"Wait," Knight said, and reached in back and pulled out a bag. He put a bottle of water in Day's hand. "Drink something and be patient. You wanted to get here early, and now you're impatient." He checked his watch and rested back in the seat.

"Why here?"

"What better place?" Knight indicated the containers. "They all look alike, and they make great hiding places. They lock and are tough enough to provide a good shelter."

"You're saying he's in there—inside one of the containers?"

"A bolt hole, yeah. No one is going to look at them twice, and there's enough space to live. I suspect it's one up near the building and he's wired it in so they don't even know he's here, but he's living off their electricity."

"So you have it all figured out," Day said as movement from the back of the lot caught his eye. He turned as the door to a container swung open slightly. A man stepped out, dressed in jeans and a checked shirt, wearing a cowboy hat. He closed the door and took three steps. Day opened the car door and got out. The man's clothes were different, and so was the hair color, judging by what Day saw sticking out of the hat, but he'd know his brother anywhere, no matter what.

"Stay here and wait for him. Give him a chance to make sure he's safe and that we're alone," Knight said.

Day stayed near the car as Stephen wound through the yard and then opened the gate. He stepped out, and Day walked closer, hearing Knight get out of the car.

"Why did you come?" Stephen asked, his expression hard.

"What the hell? You taking lessons from this one?" Day asked, thumbing toward Knight. "What the hell did you expect me to do?"

"I should have said nothing and let you worry. At least you wouldn't have gotten yourself involved in this mess." There was no heat in his voice. "Don't just stand there." Stephen closed and locked the gate, then climbed into the backseat of the car. "Let's go."

Knight climbed back inside, Day got into the car, and as soon as he closed his door, Knight backed up and pulled out.

"Okay. Here's what's going on…," Stephen began, but before he could say anything, Day turned in his seat and met his brother's stare.

"Don't you dare try to deflect anything! You owe me an explanation, and I'm going to have one, or so help me, he'll start driving north, and we won't fucking stop until we're halfway to Milwaukee. Now what the hell are you doing and what is going on? I get here and the first thing I see is you getting shot on television."

"That wasn't supposed to happen."

"I got that from Craft."

"Shit," Stephen said. "What did you tell him?"

"Nothing he didn't already know. We had figured there was something fishy when we didn't find any trace of blood, but you nearly scared me half to death."

"You went there?"

"Of course we did. We had to figure out what the hell happened and where you were," Day yelled, about ready to smack Stephen on the head. "No, you better start at the fucking beginning and tell me everything, or so help me, big brother or not, I'm going to come back there and strangle you."

"Jesus," Stephen said and turned to Knight. "Is he always like this?"

"Yes," Knight answered with a snicker.

Stephen shook his head. "Well, it's good to see you too."

Day wasn't buying it and waited.

"The Border Patrol needed help, and with all my traveling, they recruited me when you were in college. I traveled from place to place, putting out fires."

"Craft told us that," Day said.

"Yeah. Well, this was my big case. I was going to infiltrate a human trafficking ring. I'm assuming since you're here and have been looking around, you know the basics. Sanchez runs illegals across the border, but he also runs a slave ring. These people have no life when they get here. In fact, what they're running away from seems like a cakewalk once he gets into their lives. So he gets them placed in homes, and they become slaves. The pretty ones he whores out or sells outright."

"We figured out your alias," Day said.

"That was set up a while ago for the sole purpose of getting into Sanchez's organization. I did really well and managed to get close to him a few times. But I was under orders not to take him out. They needed him

122

to come to the US so he could be arrested. In Mexico, they'd never hold him—he has too much power. We have tons of proof, stacks of it, but he has power here as well."

"You mean a leak?" Knight asked.

"Yeah," Stephen admitted. "I'm not sure who it is, but I know suspicions were raised because of one. For a while I was able to slough it off as the Border Patrol passing them bad information, and they even became suspected of the leak for a while. I was hoping it could be plugged or used on our end, but no such luck." Stephen leaned forward. "Turn left here and keep going for a few miles." He watched out the back and settled into the seat after a few minutes. "Just keep moving."

"Is that why you haven't given them the information you gathered?" Day asked. "I'm assuming since it was in the cache that it hasn't been passed on. Do you not trust Craft?"

"I trust Craft pretty well. He's someone I've worked with for a few years, and he's a decent guy and nice enough, which is why he talked to you. Most Homeland Security guys would have told you to pound sand. I think Craft is okay, but I don't know who else is safe right now. I've been trying to figure that out and to let things cool off with Sanchez. I believe they think I'm dead and, they were trying to find out what I knew and who I'd told. There's a whole misinformation campaign going on right now to try to make Sanchez feel secure."

Day was trying to get his head around all of this. "I'm not sure whether to be angry with you for not telling me or proud of you for what you've been doing."

"I can take a little of both," Stephen said. "But remember, I know there's more to your job than you're telling me."

"Okay, fair enough, but why this? I thought you'd go back to school, maybe get the law degree you used to dream about. Go into real estate, like you told me."

"After all this is over, I'll do something like that. After this assignment, my undercover days are over, and I'll probably need to move on. Being two people at once gets a little old fast." Stephen paused.

"What about the girl?" Day asked, and Stephen's expression changed from cool detachment to sharp pain in a second.

"About a month ago, I encountered her coming across the border. Alicia was twenty and desperate. Her parents were gone, and she couldn't make a life away from the streets. So she wanted to come to the US, hoping for a better life. I met her while I was undercover on one of the coyote runs. Once we reached our destination, I tried to help her. She separated from the others and was 'caught.'" He made air quotes. "Craft promised he'd do what he could for her, and I thought she was safe. Alicia had an aunt in Chicago, and Craft was trying to work things out for her. Then Sanchez found out about me and hunted her down. The man seems to know fucking everything. He killed her and placed her in Clark's house. She was a fucking warning that he could get to anyone anywhere. Even people being protected by Border Patrol. The bastard. She was an innocent young woman."

"I take it you liked her?" Day said gently, and Stephen nodded. "Was she the girl you were interested in? You never gave me her name."

"Yeah. I thought once things were over, I could go to her. She liked me too, but I wanted her safe, and the rest would happen if it was supposed to." He sighed. "I guess it wasn't." Stephen sat quietly as Knight continued driving. "So let me ask you a few questions."

Day cringed inwardly.

"This is your partner, the one you went to Mexico and Europe with?" Stephen asked.

Day nodded. "We seem to work well together."

Knight scoffed. "Your brother is a complete pain in the ass. He never listens to anyone and is so stubborn...."

"Please. I have to countermand your assholeness, so give it a rest. And you are the very definition of stubborn and thinking you know everything." Day smiled and turned to Stephen. "He's still sore because I can shoot better than he can."

"Maybe, but you still have a lot to learn, newbie."

"And you think you're the one to teach me," Day challenged, glaring at Knight.

"I'll take that as a yes to my question," Stephen said with a smile in his voice.

Day turned back to Stephen. "So where do we go from here?"

"I have to decide who I'm going to tell about Sanchez's visit. He has to come. I stirred the pot up in Tucson to the point that his organization is falling apart there, and he needs to bring some order or someone else will move in, and he can't have that. I'm afraid to tell any of my contacts because I don't know who is in Sanchez's pocket, so I've been sitting on the information. But I can't do that for very much longer, or we'll completely miss our opportunity, and this is huge. Getting him will send a message that no one is untouchable."

"Are you so sure? If one viper is killed, another takes its place," Knight said, and Day nodded.

"Yes, it does. But we have to try. This is a man who ruins others' lives for his gain and fun. He thinks nothing of it," Stephen explained.

"Then what should we do, and who do we tell?" Day asked. "You can't do this alone."

"No," Stephen said. "But I can't allow you to do this with me. It's way too dangerous."

Day turned to Knight. He knew the promise he'd made, and it had just been invoked. He turned back around, staring at the floor of the car. His hands were tied. He'd given his word.

"Bullshit," Knight said forcefully. "Day's done more than you can imagine. He's resourceful, strong, and he never gives up. I'd say that's the kind of person you want to have your back." Knight turned to him. "I know he's the one I want to have mine."

Day wasn't sure what the hell that meant, but the light in Knight's eyes was something he'd longed to see almost since he'd first met him. The sadness was still there, but it was more transparent now, like a wispy cloud that still allowed the light through.

"So what do you want to do?" Knight pressed.

Stephen didn't answer, and Day basked in the light in Knight's eyes for a few more seconds.

"We need to find someone we know we can trust," Stephen said after a few moments.

"How about the detective who has been investigating the death at Clark's house? He wants to talk to you, but he doesn't think you killed her. It would have been easy to blame you and let it go at that to close his case."

125

"But we're going to need Border Patrol."

Day looked at Knight and saw that smile. "Then let's see if we can arrange a meeting: the detective, Simon, and us. Get them away from their offices and lay it on the line. The smaller the group, the better. Minimize leaks and maximize support."

"I'm pretty sure about Simon. He's...."

"The best thing you've got. We could try the FBI, but they'd bog things down and we'd be starting over," Day said. "I'm a pretty good judge of character, and Craft didn't have to help us or tell us anything. He could have turned us away."

"All right," Stephen agreed. "Where do we start?"

Day turned to Knight.

"Let's call our friend the detective and have him meet us first," Knight suggested and dug out his phone and the card. He handed them to Day, who dialed the number.

"Royerston."

"This is Dayton Ingram. I wanted to thank you for being so helpful."

"What can I do for you? Have you gotten any additional information on Mr. Clark?"

Day ignored his question. "Detective, I think it's safe to say that if you'll meet us at a secure location, we may be able to hand you a case that will make your entire career." He knew that would get him interested.

"Yeah, sure," Royerston quipped.

Stephen tapped him on the shoulder. "There's the Magpie Diner on State."

Day nodded. "I have one word for you: Sanchez."

Royerston said nothing at first.

"Be at the Magpie Diner on State in an hour. We may have the key to everything." Dayton hung up and put the phone in the carrier between the seats. "He'll be there."

"How can you be sure?" Stephen asked.

Day turned and smiled while Stephen gave directions to the diner. "I heard the hunger in his voice. That is a guy who wants more than what he has now." Day turned to Knight. He knew that feeling very well.

Longing for what he didn't have had driven most of Day's life since his parents' deaths.

Other than Stephen's directions, they remained quiet while Knight drove across the city.

When they arrived at the diner, the three of them went inside, and Day walked up to where the detective sat in a booth facing the door. "This is my brother."

"Mr. Miller," Detective Royerston said as he stood and extended his hand.

"Actually, that's quite a long story," Stephen said as he shook hands. "Maybe we should sit down, and I can tell you part of it quickly before we get down to business." He motioned Day inside and then slid into the outside position of the booth.

"Why are we here?" Royerston asked. "And why shouldn't I take you in for questioning?"

"We're here because my brother and Knight believe you can be trusted." Stephen's gaze bored heated holes into the detective. Day half expected his white shirt to burst into flames. "Clark Miller is an alias set up by Border Patrol and Homeland Security. The thing is, there's a leak there. I'm sure of it."

Royerston nodded. "Doesn't surprise me. Sanchez has a lot of people in his pocket. I'm not one of them." The indignation in his voice and eyes rang true.

"Good, because Sanchez is planning to come to the US, specifically to Tucson. Because of his status, a visit like his takes a lot of planning, and he wants to remain out of the hands of the authorities. My cover was compromised, and my superiors thought it would be best if Sanchez thought I was dead."

"We believe they think he is, but we also think they're wondering what information he might have had. So we've been followed," Knight explained.

"Word has it that Border Patrol is interested in you two as well. At least some faction is," Royerston said. "In certain circles you two have made quite a name for yourselves."

"So you think the leak is real?" Stephen asked.

"There have been rumors for years. Nothing concrete, but good arrests seem to fall through. So yeah...." He seemed resigned. "There's too much power in the hands of people who shouldn't have it."

The waitress approached, a pot of coffee in her hand, and filled thick ceramic mugs on the table for each of them.

"Then what do you suggest?"

"I can provide where he's going to be and most likely when," Stephen said. "But I'm hoping you know reliable people who aren't in Sanchez's pocket. I don't think my boss at Border Patrol is bad, but I don't know who might be compromised there. I'll contact him and make him promise to tell no one else in the organization. He has a private cell phone, so I'll use that."

"Then what?" Royerston asked.

"Then you guys have to do your jobs," Stephen said, "and not let Sanchez slip through your fingers."

"You'll walk away," Royerston asked. "Just like that—let someone else have the credit for taking out the biggest human trafficker in the country?" He seemed shocked.

"All that counts is that we get him, and that he doesn't escape back across the border. Once you have him, you can get a lot of his generals and decapitate the organization."

"He isn't going to talk," Royerston said. "These guys never do."

"Maybe not. But follow the paper trail. Sanchez has a good one if you know where to look. I have notes on his organization as well, including who reports to whom and who is in charge of each area. Taking them out is going to put him out of business and stop an easy leadership transition."

"Okay. I'm with you. I have close contacts in Tucson. I can work with them."

Stephen nodded. He looked really tired. "This is life or death—you know that."

Royerston nodded and sipped his coffee. "I know and I'll treat it that way." He checked his watch. "I better not sit here too long or there will be questions as to why I'm away. You contact your boss, and we'll meet tomorrow. Just let me know when and where. You'll need to bring whatever information you have." Royerston stood and placed some money on the table before striding out of the diner.

Stephen watched him go. "Do you really think we can trust him?"

"I hope so," Day said, looking at Knight for his opinion.

Knight nodded slowly. "He's a lawman through and through. I think he wants to get Sanchez as badly as anyone. He sees what the trade in illegals is doing to his city and the state, and if he can stem the flow for a while, it will help his city." Knight drained his mug. "We need to get out of here. There isn't any cover, and there are way too many windows. They served our purpose, but now they're a problem." Knight slid out of the booth and left some additional cash on the table. Then he waited for Stephen and Day before pushing outside and hurrying to the car.

"Where do you want us to take you?" Day asked once the car doors had closed. "And please don't say back to the shipping container." He wrinkled his nose. "I wasn't going to say anything, but I'm willing to bet that thing doesn't come with a shower." He turned to Knight. "There are rooms in the hotel, and we'll get you there with us. Safety in numbers."

"There isn't anyone watching you?" Stephen asked.

"We pretty much gave everyone the slip. The only exposure was coming to see you." Knight took evasive action in case they were followed, and they went back to the Comfort Inn. "I'm going to get another room. Day, take Stephen to our room. He can take a shower and borrow some clothes. Then I think we all need to talk."

Day led Stephen in through the back door and up the stairs. Inside the room, he checked for listening devices, even though it didn't seem like anyone had been there. "Here are some clothes. It's just a T-shirt and shorts. I wasn't planning on it taking this long to find you." Day pushed the clothes into Stephen's hands and turned away.

"Don't be petulant," Stephen chided.

"Fuck you, Stephen," Day said with more heat than he intended. "Just go get your shower."

"What's gotten into you?"

"You're in trouble and you send some stupid note about being in trouble and to stay away. If you're in trouble, who the hell else are you going to call? Ghostbusters? Me. I'm your brother, the only family you have, and you shut me out."

"I don't see you calling me when things happen." Stephen set the clothes on the desk. "We're not kids anymore. You have a dangerous job that you can't talk about. And I'm sorry, but I have… or had… one, too, that I couldn't talk about. That isn't the best basis for open communication. Besides, you have someone who has your back. You don't need me for that any longer." He turned toward the door.

"Who watches your back?" Day asked.

"I'm used to watching my own," Stephen said, turning back to Day. "Undercover work is solitary and dangerous. I knew that going in, but I love it. I know I lied to you about my life for a long time, and I'm sorry about that. You of all people should have been told the truth. It would have made things easier on both of us."

Day heard the key in the door, and Stephen picked up the clothes and went into the bathroom as Knight entered the room. He closed the door, and Day stared at him until Knight did the unexpected: he walked over to Day and pulled him into his arms. He didn't say anything at first, but he was there.

"I got the room next door for him," Knight whispered. "Did the two of you talk?"

"Yeah. I hadn't realized how much things had changed while I was busy."

"You were living your life, and so was he. What happened was probably normal because of distance and time. Things change and that's okay."

Day found himself smiling at the thought of Knight as the relationship expert.

"If we're going to hunker down for a while, I think I need to get some food, and you should check in with Dimato to make sure the world hasn't fallen apart. He might have some advice as well." Day grabbed a room key and his phone, along with the glasses and hat Knight had him wear as a disguise. Not that he thought a determined watcher would be fooled, but it never hurt to take precautions from the casual observer.

"Be careful. Now that we've found Stephen and know some of what's going on, we're even more vulnerable and exposed," Knight said as Day reached for the doorknob. "Before, we couldn't reveal what we didn't know, but now...." He looked at the bathroom door, and Day understood.

They had everything in their hands—all the information they needed to end this. That was usually the point when they made a mad dash across Europe with the Russians on their tail, or hightailed it out of Mexico after leaving a wake of destruction, one of them with bullet wounds. Things had a tendency to go to hell at this point.

"I'll take my phone and text every few minutes so you know it's okay," Day said before opening the door. He thought Knight might be overreacting, but taking chances wasn't a good thing.

The door banged closed, and Day half jogged down the hall and the stairs, then exited the hotel, glancing around before walking across the parking lot toward the restaurants and convenience stores clustered nearby.

I'm going to stop at the Mini Mart and then get burgers, Day texted as he walked toward the convenience store. It seemed a little nuts. He didn't see anyone paying any attention to him, and there were no familiar faces.

Inside, he grabbed some snacks, remembering that Knight liked Cheetos and that his brother had an unnatural fascination with Twinkies. Day shuddered as he grabbed a package. He got some water and soda, then carried his haul to the register, where he paid. When he left, he texted that he was going to Burger King for dinner. More than anything, he wanted food that wasn't fast and tasted like something, but this was the best they were going to get for now.

No onions, Knight sent back, and Day rolled his eyes. He knew that.

He dropped his phone into his pocket, kept his hand there, and crossed the access road between the businesses. A car slowed and made the turn. Day hurried across so he wouldn't get hit and was grabbed from behind and thrown into the car, hitting his head on the top of the door. He struggled as a man climbed on top of him, holding him down. The car door slammed closed, and they started moving.

"This isn't the one we want," a gruff voice said.

"Who cares? It's one of them, and he'll lead us to the others or I'll skin him alive."

The voice sent chills up Day's spine. He closed his eyes and pulled his phone from his pocket, slipping it between the seats.

As he opened his mouth to protest, his gaze caught sight of a gun heading toward his face. Pain bloomed, and then blackness.

Chapter 8

STEPHEN CAME out of the bathroom wearing some of Day's clothes.

"Feeling better?" Knight asked as Stephen set the pile of dirty clothes to the side.

"Human."

"Day went to get some food."

Stephen turned his head as he took in the room. "What's going on with you and my brother?"

"Direct, aren't you?" Knight said, a little surprised, but preferring a straight shooter.

"Works best," Stephen said. "I know you're his work partner, and he's told me that there's been… other interactions between you. And I want to know your intentions."

Knight chuckled at the term. "My intentions?"

Stephen stalked over. "Are you just fucking with him or is there more? He's been through a lot and deserves someone who isn't going to jerk him around."

"I think that's his business."

Stephen didn't turn away. "I've been with you two for a couple of hours now, and I see the way he looks at you and the way you look at him. I know there's something between you, but I can't figure it out. You bicker like an old married couple and jab at each other in a comfortable way. I can also tell you trust each other."

"Then what's the problem?" Knight asked as his discomfort level rose quickly.

"Day is independent. I raised him as well as I could after our parents died, and he's independent and strong after going through hell and back."

Knight sighed. "He isn't the only one who's been through shit," he growled. "Believe it or not, your brother and I do talk about more than work. I know what happened to him, and he knows about my past."

133

He had no intention of going into that with Stephen, but as he watched, he saw understanding that could only mean Day had shared with him. Knight wasn't sure how he felt about that.

"Don't worry. Day only speaks in the broadest terms when he talks about you. But he did tell me you had a wife and son. Is that what's holding you back?"

Knight got to his feet. "What the hell is with you? Everything is fine, and I don't think this is any of your business." He stalked toward the bathroom. "How can you know any of this unless Day has been running his mouth?"

"I have eyes. At the diner he barely looked at anyone but you except when they were speaking. It was like the two of you were communicating without saying a word to each other. I know what that kind of connection means, because my parents had it. I remember knowing if I was in trouble by the way they looked at each other, zings of energy shooting between them. It was freaky, and I see the same between you two, except you're holding back. I took a guess that it had something to do with your family."

"I can't believe I'm having this conversation. In fact, I'm not. It's over. If I want to talk about this shit, I'll do it with Day."

"Yeah," Stephen said and sat back in his chair. "I bet the two of you sit around, knitting socks, talking about your feelings until the estrogen blooms all over the room. You two live on guts, action, and testosterone, and it flies thick and heavy most of the time. Hell, I do too, but I'm alone."

"Yeah, it's a shame about that girl. Alicia."

"My cover got out of hand. It happens sometimes," Stephen said.

Knight nodded. He could imagine things getting carried away. He'd wondered more than once if he hadn't let things with Day get carried away.

"So what's the real issue?"

"Fuck off. You think I'm going to talk about stuff like that with you?" He didn't talk about crap like this with anyone, not even Day, and he wasn't going to bring it up with Day's brother.

"Fine. Then I'll guess."

"You're a pushy bastard, aren't you?" Knight said.

"Don't get anywhere otherwise." Stephen was so relaxed, Knight wanted to walk over and smash him in the face. "I know you lost your wife and son. You think that if you let someone else in your life, you'll be letting go of them. That they'll be less important in your life and will fade away." Stephen's gaze bored into him, and Knight didn't dare move. There was no way in hell he could let on that Stephen's shot was too close to the center of the target for words. "You know things don't work that way."

"How do you know anything about this?" Knight demanded. "Have you ever lost a wife and child?" Knight's anger bubbled up and was near to exploding; his hands clenched into fists.

"I know plenty. How large was the family you came from?"

"Pretty big, I guess."

"So you have brothers and sisters?" Stephen asked.

Knight nodded and wondered where Stephen was going with this.

"Your parents loved all of you, right?"

He nodded again, taking the simplest answer rather than going into family drama. "I'm the oldest."

"Perfect." Stephen smiled, and Knight wanted to slap it off his face. "So when you were born, your parents loved you, and what happened when the next child was born? Did they pull that love away and transfer it to the new baby?"

"Of course not. They loved her too."

"Exactly," Stephen said as he slowly got to his feet. "If you really care for Day the way he cares for you, then you need to expand your heart so that there's room for him as well as your wife and son. He isn't going to replace them." Stephen grinned as though he'd won some contest, and Knight snatched up his phone because he had to do something other than want to kill Day's brother.

He checked his messages and the times. "Something's wrong." He sent a *Where are you?* message, but didn't get a response. "Shit." He opened the tracking application Day had installed on his phone, logged in, and swore one more time. "We need to go. Day's a few blocks away and moving." He yanked open the door and exploded into the hallway without waiting for Stephen. He was already halfway down the hall before the door closed, Stephen racing after him.

Knight took the stairs two at a time and nearly tripped as he reached the bottom. He leaped to the car, started the engine, and pulled out as soon as Stephen closed the passenger door. "Hang the hell on." He tossed his phone to Stephen. "Tell me where they're going."

"Shouldn't we call someone?" Stephen asked.

"No time. Day is getting farther away, and if Sanchez's people have him, you know every second counts." *Shit.* Knight gripped the wheel, floored the accelerator, and weaved through traffic like a madman. He figured if he picked up any police, he could deal with them once he caught up with Day.

"They're stopped ahead. Maybe they don't want to draw attention to themselves so they aren't driving like they have a death wish."

Knight smiled at the squeak in Stephen's voice as he swerved hard around a soccer mom's minivan and kept moving.

"Less than a mile now, and they're moving again. You might want to slow down so they don't see you coming like a bat out of hell."

Knight turned off the main road. "Just tell me where they are," he said and made a right turn, flew down an alley, across another street where he narrowly missed a truck, and darted down yet another alley. "I hope you have good control of your faculties."

"So do I," Stephen said. "They're just ahead, moving parallel to us. Three more blocks ought to do it, and then we'll be ahead of them." Stephen's voice trembled, but Knight ignored it. All he could think about was getting Day back. Nothing else mattered at the moment. "What are you going to do?"

He made the turn with the car on two wheels, then slammed back down onto the pavement as he raced to the intersection. "Where are they?"

"Just approaching the intersection." Stephen pointed. "That has to be them."

"Hang on!" Knight floored the accelerator, the car leaping forward. He was never so thankful that an intersection was otherwise empty as he rammed the front of the rental into the back of the Cadillac. Metal screeched and bent, ripping, tearing. Plastic broke, and shards of glass and bits of car body flew everywhere, the pieces moving in slow motion for a fraction of a second. The Cadillac spun around, and Knight's rental spun as well, the airbag popping and deflating. Knight brought his car under control and to a stop. There wasn't much left of the front end, but the door worked, and he jumped out and raced across the pavement.

The Cadillac was another story. The driver had lost control, and it had crashed into a parked car. Knight could smell fuel as he approached. The driver's side rested against what was left of a red Escort. The passenger door opened, and Knight reached for the man as he got out, pulled him to the pavement, stamped his foot in the center of his back, and grabbed the gun that fell to the ground. "Where's the man you took?"

"Knight," Stephen called as he pulled open the back door and got Day out.

"What the hell happened?" Day asked, and Knight's heart instantly returned to a more normal rhythm.

"Knight got a little overzealous in his attempt to get you back," Stephen said.

"You need to get the police here. The others in the car aren't doing so well," Day said as he slid to the ground.

"Are you okay?" Knight asked. "That's all that matters. The rest of them can bleed out for all I care." He kicked the guy on the ground when he tried to move.

"You crazy man," he groaned.

"And you're about as stupid as they come." Knight leaned a little closer. "You idiots have no idea who you're dealing with." He turned to Day. "Are you really okay?"

"Yeah. I'd be better if my partner wasn't so damned reckless." He rubbed the back of his neck. "They had me flat on the seat, so I was cushioned in the impact."

"We tracked your phone, but I'm wondering why they didn't disable it." The scent of fuel hung in the air, and Knight knew they needed to get the hell away.

"I hid it," Day said and reached into the car.

"What the hell are you doing? Get the hell away from that thing."

Day pulled away and held up his phone. He got to his feet and moved away from the car.

Knight did the same, dragging the guy on the ground with him like a doll.

The explosion ripped through the air, sending them all flat on the ground. Knight's ears rang, but he kept a bead on the guy he pulled from the car as heat washed over him. When he could see again, Day and Stephen were behind him, with Stephen talking on the phone.

"Royerston is on his way."

Knight looked around as a crowd began to gather. "Get the hell away from here. Other cars could blow." He showed the gun, and that was enough to send people scattering. He muttered under his breath as sirens sounded. This was going to get damned messy. Knight had to think fast. "Stephen, make yourself scarce. The last thing we need is your face on the news. Day, call Dimato to make sure we have political backup." This situation could spin out of control dang fast.

The crowd of onlookers grew again, and Stephen was able to meld into them and then disappear. The police arrived en masse, and Knight set the gun on the ground, stepped away, and submitted to them without a struggle. Once Royerston arrived, he felt much better.

"Let him up," Royerston said as he approached the officer who was holding him on the ground.

"He had a gun to him," the young officer said, indicating one of Day's kidnappers, who had already half talked the officer into believing that Knight had been the attacker and that he and his dead friends were innocent, complete with a sniffle and a tear.

"What happened?" Royerston asked once Knight got to his feet.

"They nabbed Day near the hotel. I was able to track them because Day was as smart as anything and hid his phone in the seat. I crashed into them to keep them from getting away and the car exploded."

"There are two others in the car, or what's left of it," Day said. "The driver and the guy holding me didn't stand a chance with Reckless Mabel here." He smiled, and Knight rolled his eyes. "He did what he had to do."

"Take him into custody," Royerston said fiercely, pointing to the kidnapper. "I want him held. Contact no one, and if he tries to lawyer up, he can have one… eventually. Get him out of here now and back to the station, in a cell. I don't want him walking."

The kidnapper began to yell in Spanish.

"Shut him up," Royerston said, and the officers hustled the guy into a car.

Knight turned away, not wanting to witness how they kept him quiet.

"Where's the other in your group?"

"I thought it best if he wasn't around in case there were news cameras," Knight answered quietly. "We can't let this stop what's more important. This was one hell of an accident. There were two deaths, but what if we report that there were three and that Stephen Ingram from the pursuing car was also killed? That should put Sanchez and his people at ease."

"That's who they were trying to get at," Day added as he joined their huddle. "They said I was the wrong guy but could be used to get who they wanted."

Royerston shook his head. "You guys sure play fast and loose with the truth." He sighed loudly. "You know I could be busted down to beat cop for this, but I'll take care of it. I have contacts who can pass some information where it needs to go."

"Tell your captain what's going on, if you're sure you can trust him. But Sanchez is too big a fish to let anything get in the way." Knight looked at Day, who nodded. He couldn't look away. Knight let his gaze rake over Dayton, looking for injury or anything wrong. More than anything he wanted to get him back to the hotel so he could check him over very closely and personally.

Fire trucks arrived and began dousing the burning car, though the fire had already begun to die down because most of the fuel had been consumed. No one other than the men in the Cadillac seemed to have been injured, but the owner of the old Escort, a college-age woman, was very upset about the loss of her car. Knight made sure Royerston got her information, figuring that anonymous help could be sent her way if needed.

"You both need to come back to the station," Royerston told them once the fire was under control and he had taken statements. "This has to look like a severe traffic incident."

"It's not like we have transportation," Day said and turned to what was left of the rental. "We're going to have plenty of explaining to do to the boss."

Knight snickered. "I think I'll leave that to you. He likes you better than me," Knight said as they got in the back of the police cruiser.

Day bumped his shoulder as he joined him. "Everyone likes me better than they do you. I'm a nice guy. You're an asshole."

"It seems like you're none the worse for wear if you can give me grief."

"I was pretty protected, but you didn't know that," Day scolded.

Knight turned in the seat as Royerston got in the car. "All I knew was that if we lost you, I wasn't going to be able to find you in time. These men weren't going to be making phone calls with ransom demands. They were going to get the information they wanted out of you any way they could, and then that would be the end of you. I knew I was taking a chance, but I had to stop them, and the only weapon I had was the car."

"Okay, you two," Royerston snapped. "What the hell happened?"

"They must have followed a trail to the hotel," Knight explained. "I don't know how because we were careful after leaving the diner." He blew air through his nose in frustration. "Sometimes I think these people are idiots, and then they pull something like that and take me by surprise." He ground his teeth. "I hate being snuck up on."

"So what's this idea of yours? And where is his brother?"

"That we don't know. He'll be in touch, I hope," Day answered, his nerves clear. "But Knight's right. We need to report that my brother died in the crash. If Sanchez believes it, he might continue with his trip."

"If I were Sanchez, I'd stay the hell away," Royerston said. "Things have got to feel hot to him."

"I'm sure they do," Knight said, leaning forward. "But his organization is feeling a lot of heat, and he's going to want to put an end to the fraying, pull things back together so he can keep the money flowing. Tucson is a mess, and now Phoenix is becoming a problem. Muscle and power are all that these people understand. He's going to come in town, meet with his people, including the officials on his payroll, dispense justice at the point of a gun, and instill fear that will have everyone hopping. It's what these guys do."

"True. He can't sit by while things go to hell, or his entire organization will come apart," Royerston agreed.

Knight turned to Day and then leaned closer to Royerston. "If I were him, I'd be adding a stop in Phoenix to my little agenda. You might want to check airports, especially the smaller ones, for last-minute flights. He isn't going to use the major airports, but he will arrive in style to put on a show." He sat back and thought for a few minutes.

"He may be wanted, but his organization needs to think he's invincible and owns every inch of ground he walks on," Day said.

"Jesus, you two sound like some FBI guys I worked with a few years ago. I swore they could crawl into people's heads."

"Nope. Just thinking like a scumbag," Day said with a smile before touching his head.

Knight leaned closer and gently took a look. "You're bleeding," he whispered. "We need to get that cleaned up."

"The dead asshole in the back coldcocked me. I managed to catch a glancing blow and pretended to be out while they drove. I figured letting them think I wasn't a threat would give me an advantage. Turned out I didn't need one."

"Hiding your phone in the seat was a stroke of genius," Knight said. "They searched you and must have thought you didn't have one. Weren't they watching you text?"

"I put it away before I left the store. They must have thought I dropped it when they grabbed me. Assumptions will get you in trouble every time."

"Speaking of trouble...," Royerston said as they pulled into the police station. "That's my captain, Grantham Jacobs, and he never waits for someone to come in, so I suspect he's either about ready to explode or has already blown a hole in the roof of his office."

"Shit," Knight groaned. "I guess we need to face the music."

"Royerston," Jacobs seethed as he came down the steps of the stone building. "I take it these are the two who have been making a mess of my city."

"Actually, that would be Carlos Sanchez, and we're trying to help you take care of him," Day said, standing toe to toe with the large, fuming police captain. "You might want to take this inside before something happens."

"What have I said before about kicking the bear?" Knight asked in a whisper. "He's the bear."

"You better believe it," Jacobs said. "Now get inside. All three of you, in my office. Now." He pointed, and Knight waited for Royerston to lead them in.

"Sorry if we got you in trouble," Knight said under his breath to Royerston.

"I'm only in real trouble if this shit falls through. Then I'll be walking a beat again… or worse," Royerston said.

They weaved through the station, around desks, and to an office. The place seemed as though it had seen better days. Prolonged budget issues and other stretched resources had taken their toll during the downturn.

"Okay," Captain Jacobs snapped after the door smacked closed. "What the hell is going on?"

Knight intended to let Royerston do the talking, but he stood quiet, so Knight stepped forward. "A foiled kidnapping—two of Sanchez's men are dead and one is in custody. You also have the chance to take him down. Things got a little messy, but I couldn't let them take my partner. That wasn't going to happen." Knight met Jacobs's glare measure for measure. "Any more questions?"

"Don't mind him," Day said from where he stood next to Knight. "He can be a bit of an ass."

"So your boss told me. It seems you two have cut quite a swath over the past few days. Visiting a crime scene, meeting with desert coyotes, traveling hours to visit yet another crime scene. Taking up police resources, high-speed chases, a highway shooting…. Did I miss anything? You two are turning out to be the belles of the ball."

"You forgot muscling Homeland Security," Day said and turned to Knight. "Though that was more fun than anything else."

"Those guys are strung way too tight," Knight said, and he thought the captain's head was going to explode.

"It's pretty simple," Day began. "My brother was the man shot on television a few days ago. I knew he was in trouble, but not why.

We followed his trail and found him, but it turned out that he wasn't exactly what I thought he was. He has information on an upcoming visit by Sanchez to the US—Tucson and now possibly Phoenix—as well as the entire organization. They want him dead, and he wasn't sure who he could trust, even inside Homeland. Royerston is a stand-up officer, and after dealing with him, we believed he could be trusted, so we contacted him for help."

"This isn't about turf or glory. It's about getting Sanchez," Knight added.

Jacob's expression softened slightly. "Son of a bitch."

"Exactly. So do you want him or not?" Day snapped, and Knight kept the pride off his face.

"Where is this information?" Captain Jacobs asked.

"My brother has it," Day said.

This was where things got sticky.

"And where is your brother?" Captain Jacobs asked, looking around.

Knight nodded, telling Day he'd take over. "He was with me in the car, but he melted into the crowd and took off. They were after him, so we let them think he's dead. Stephen will contact Day, and we'll be able to get the information we need. We know he's going to be in Tucson—Stephen pretty much made sure of that—but with the mess going on here, we think he'll need to show his authority to his people in Phoenix."

"What is your plan for all this?"

"To hand you the information and let you run with it," Knight answered. "All we want is Sanchez out of the way and his organization brought to an end. That way Stephen might be able to show his face again. To do that, we have to capture him in this country. Mexico can't hold him."

"No, they can't," Captain Jacobs agreed. "What about the feds?"

"Stephen believes they can't be trusted either. He believes someone in Border Patrol is a leak. So that's why he's been hiding, trying to figure out who he can trust."

"And you two chose us?" Jacobs asked.

Knight nodded.

"Good choice," Jacobs said. "I've wanted to get that bastard since my first homicide investigation. He was involved, but I couldn't touch him." He straightened up. "We'll take it from here as long as you pass on the information we need." Jacobs leaned over his desk. "Don't make me go into what will happen if you don't."

A knock sounded and then the door cracked open. A young female officer stuck her head in. "There's a man out front, says he needs to talk to Royerston about some information he has. Says his name's Clark Miller."

"The missing brother, I presume?" Jacobs asked.

Day nodded to Captain Jacobs, and he motioned to Royerston, who closed the door. They all waited until Stephen was escorted into the office, holding the notebook they'd found in the locked box in Stephen's yard.

"This is the key to Sanchez's organization." Stephen laid the notebook on the captain's desk. "I compiled this information over months. It's got the names of leaders, operatives, people on the payroll, and information about a planned trip, but I suspect those plans will have been altered." Stephen spoke softly and looked tired. "I want this to be over. These two think that your department can be trusted, and I hope to hell that's true. Otherwise the one chance we have to get this guy will be gone."

"What about calling Simon?"

Stephen shook his head. "Simon was killed in a drive-by shooting this morning on his way to work. Homeland Security is going to be paralyzed for a while. They'll be looking for revenge and tearing themselves apart trying to figure out how this could happen. Meanwhile their eyes will be focused internally while Sanchez makes his visit."

Captain Jacobs sat back in his seat. "So you're saying the biggest case to hit this area in years is sitting right on my desk."

"Yup."

"Royerston, you're in charge. Get started digging into what you can. We need to know what the word is, and if this Sanchez visit is really going to happen. I'd like to think that our department is clean, but there's too much money involved for me to be certain of that. So be careful who you include."

"Yes, sir."

"As for these three, get them to a safe hotel. They look about ready to fall over." He smiled for the first time.

"We need to get our things, and it would be best if we didn't draw attention to ourselves," Knight said, knowing it wasn't likely they were going to be in control of anything any longer.

"Royerston will take you and get you somewhere safe. After that, you'll sit tight and wait." He shook his head. "It would be just like you to get involved, and we don't need additional complications. This is a police matter now." He turned his gaze to Royerston, and Knight knew arguing would be futile. Not that he really minded.

Royerston led them out of the office to an unmarked car, then drove to their hotel. They were all quiet as they rode. Knight sat next to Day and kept looking at him, just to make sure he was all right. They got their things at the hotel, and then Royerston drove them to a small motel at the edge of town.

It looked like something out of another age, with wooden cacti decorating the front of the building and horse cutouts in the circle drive. The forties and fifties were definitely alive and well at the Desert Dreams Motel.

They got the keys to the rooms, and Royerston stopped in to his and Day's room to say good-bye. "You should be safe here. This is far enough off the beaten path that no one will look here."

"Why do I feel like we're being hidden away?" Day asked.

"Sanchez and his people know about you. If you want to be safe, you have to stay out of sight. You guys did the heavy lifting on this, and it won't be forgotten." Royerston stepped closer. "I'll let you know when things are going down. You deserve to be in on the action if you want, but for now, you're the ones in danger. The kidnapping told us all that."

Day sighed and shook Royerston's hand before turning to Knight. "We could just get on a plane and go home."

He looked tired, and once Royerston left, Knight guided Day to the bed. When he'd stretched out, Knight pulled off his shoes and socks and then unbuttoned Day's shirt. Black and blue marks spotted Day's chest from Knight's little escapade to try to rescue him.

"What are you doing?" Day asked.

"I need to see that you're okay," Knight whispered. He went into the bathroom and wetted a cloth, then came back, bringing along a towel. He carefully cleaned the blood out of Day's hair.

"I'm fine. There's no need to fuss. It doesn't suit you." Day stood and took off his shirt. "Knight is hard and a pain in the ass. He doesn't do gentle very well, and when he does, it's because he's had too much to drink or is feeling guilty about something."

"Or maybe it's because he's realized he was a fool," Knight said, and Day whipped around, wincing slightly. A knock on the door interrupted them, and Knight unlocked the door after checking who was outside.

"Hey, guys," Stephen said as he walked in the room.

Knight returned to Day's side after locking the door, staying still. He knew Stephen was aware of things between them, but having him see the two of them together was unexpected and a little uncomfortable. "What?" Knight growled and moved in front of Day.

"Royerston said he was going to bring some food before he went back to the station. I wasn't sure which room, but he can bring it to mine." Stephen had the good sense to close the door as he left, and Knight returned his attention to what was truly important.

"You were saying you were a fool," Day prompted.

"You would remember that."

Day smiled. "Remember it? I'm going to mark it on my calendar and celebrate it each year as a holiday." He winced again as Knight began removing the rest of his clothes. "So what were you being a fool about?" Day lifted his hips, and Knight got Day's pants down and carefully pulled them off his legs.

"Do you really want me to go into it?" Knight asked, hoping Day would give him a reprieve. "Your brother and I had a talk just before I realized you were missing, and I figured out that I've been stupid and holding on to the wrong things."

"You're going to have to explain this to me." Day slid up on the bed and lay on his back, sighing softly. "Damn, that feels good. My back isn't particularly happy after being tumbled around." He lifted his head. "I think you need to be barred from driving for a while. Have you gone a little crazy? That stunt could have killed me."

Knight shivered. "That wasn't my intention. All I could think about was you getting away and not being able to find you. I hoped like hell you would have known I'd come after you once you left a trail to follow."

"Okay, I get that. But ramming the car…." Day groaned and dropped his head back down to the pillow, relaxing and finally closing his eyes.

"I'd just realized that it wasn't an either/or. That I could have my memories of Cheryl and Zachary and still let you in my life, and then you were fucking kidnapped, and I was determined to get you back so I could tell you. And now I have, and you're giving me a hard time about it."

"You nearly killed me. I think I have a license to give you grief about that for some time to come. So I think you should get used to it," Day said with a smile. "And I'm glad you figured some things out."

"That's all you have to say?" Knight asked, a little shocked. This was a huge step for him, and Day was acting as though it were nothing.

Day shrugged and Knight leaned closer. Day smiled at him and drew Knight down just so their lips nearly touched. "I know what that means, and I know you do too."

Knight climbed onto the bed to be nearer to him. He wanted to get even closer. Day reached for his shirt and tugged it up over Knight's head. "I don't think Stephen is going to be in any hurry to return." He cut off Day's chuckle with a kiss. For the first time since letting down his guard around Day, the push and pull between his past and the present was absent.

Day wrapped his arms around Knight's neck, tugging him closer.

Knight had always thought there were times when talking was overrated, and intimate time with Day more than proved it. Lips were meant for kissing and tasting. He let his hands do the talking. He had to know Day was truly all right.

He started at Day's chest, cupping his pecs, muscles ripping under his palms. "I'm sorry if I hurt you. I saw red, and all I could think about was stopping them."

"So the thought of losing me was enough to shoot past that Marine reserve and calm of yours," Day said with a smile. "You know, I think I like that. Even if the result was dangerous and majorly reckless."

147

"All I could think about was what would happen to you if they got away." He'd finally realized he could let Day into his life without losing the others who mattered to him, and then Day had been taken away. He hadn't been able to bear that.

"Well, they didn't, thanks to you."

Knight leaned closer, and Day groaned. Knight stopped, and Day held him closer, sliding his hands down his back, slipping into Knight's pants to cup his ass. Day squeezed and pressed them together, moaning softly into the kiss. As Day worked his hands around to the front of Knight's pants, he held his breath. Day parted the fabric and then shoved them down Knight's legs. He kicked them off, along with his shoes, holding himself over Day by his extended arms. The bruises on Day's hip and arm made him wince, and the cut on his head nearly had Knight seeing red once again.

"Sometimes I think we need to find a safer job," Knight said.

"Tell me about it," Day groaned, pushing his hips upward, sliding their cocks together. He pulled Knight's hips down and slid his hands up Knight's side lightly enough that Knight squirmed, seconds away from a tickled laugh. "I'm fine. They didn't really hurt me, and you came to my rescue."

Knight was grateful the teasing seemed to have stopped. Day kissed him, and Knight rolled them on the seventies orange-and-brown bedspread to keep his weight from crushing Day. He'd already come close to hurting him, and he'd never do that again.

"What do you want, Knight?" Day asked as he squirmed and groaned in a show of delight that Knight wondered how he'd managed to do without.

"Whatever you want," Knight answered as he realized that making Day happy meant more than his own happiness. That was the moment, the lightbulb realization of just how much he cared for the man lying on top of him, whose skin was as hot as lava and made his heart ache and burn in a way it never had before. "You're what's important. I see that now. It isn't me and all my issues. It's you."

"No. See, when you care for someone, it isn't me and you any longer, it becomes us. That's what my mother told me. It was one of the last things she said. Don't know why, and it seemed strange at the time, but…." Day smiled. "I remember. I asked her how she knew she loved Daddy, and she said it was when she started thinking about 'us,' the two of them, rather than herself."

"When did that happen to you?" Knight asked, wrapping his legs around Day's, wanting to be as close and have as many points of contact as possible. The hotel room was warm and getting hotter by the second, but Knight didn't care. He had Day in his arms, a whole and mostly healthy Day.

"When you were shot and in bad shape. I knew how much I cared, but you weren't ready to hear that or deal with it. So I kept it to myself and hoped you'd come around." Day leaned forward to lick and bite at Knight's neck. "I think the time for talking is over for now. If I know Stephen, he's going to be knocking in about fifteen minutes because he'll be ready to eat, and the end result is that either there will be nothing left or he's going to barge in here."

"So you're saying there's a time limit."

"I'm saying that we should make the most of the quiet and work at making a little noise." He grinned mischievously.

"Honey, I know I can make you scream." Knight massaged up and down Day's chest, then trailed his fingers down his ripped belly, caressing him slowly, loving the way Day's eyes drifted closed and his back arched. "You are amazing to look at." He stroked faster, Day rolling his hips. That sight was gorgeous and took his breath away.

Knight pulled Day down to him, guiding their lips together. He could kiss him all day and all night, for hours on end. Day always tasted like warm summer air, heat, and a hint of cinnamon that Knight knew came from his toothpaste.

Day trembled in his arms. "We don't have anything…."

Knight slid his hands down Day's back, groaning when they slipped over the curve of his hard ass and then over the smooth cheeks. He could hold on to this forever. No one was as wonderful or as perfect as Day. Now that he'd opened himself to the possibility of Day in his life, he didn't want to let go. This was happiness, and his spirit was light for the first time in many years. "I love how you feel in my hands."

"And I love when I'm buried deep inside you and I touch that spot that makes your mouth fall open and your eyes roll in your head," Day said.

"So is that what you want?" Knight asked.

"I don't know what I want or what I can do right now," Day answered, and Knight nodded, smiled, and gripped Day's throbbing cock.

"How about this?" Knight asked. "Lie back on the bed, close your eyes, and let me take care of you." Knight stilled and felt the shiver of desire run through Day. Damn, that was hot. Just a few words had Day breathing short and fast.

Day nodded and moved slowly until he was lying sprawled out on the spread.

Knight climbed off the bed and stood next to it, looking at Day. He didn't move for a while, taking him in.

"I thought you were going to take care of me."

"I will." Knight raked his gaze down Day's chest, following the lines on his belly to the divot of his hip and then down to where his legs joined his body. Knight cupped Day's balls, rolling them gently in his fingers while Day's cock bounced up and down on his belly. "Is this better?" He leaned forward, climbing on the bed, and took Day's cock between his lips, sucking him slowly into his mouth.

"Holy God!" Day cried, thrusting his hips upward.

Knight hummed as Day's flavor filled his mouth. This was intense, intimate, and special. He and Day had had sex plenty of times, but something was different now. His heart was light.... Hell, now it was engaged. He was feeling Day with more than his hands, tasting him with more than his lips. Every sensation sank deep inside. He took Day in, inhaling his rich musky scent as he did.

"More, please, for God's sake, don't you dare stop," Day groaned as he quivered on the bed.

Knight bobbed his head, loving the feel of Day's cock sliding along his tongue. He was quickly realizing that everything about Day turned him on. He ran his hand up Day's belly and then his chest, rolling a nipple between his fingers, listening as Day's soft moans grew louder and more urgent. "I love how responsive you are," Knight whispered after letting Day slip from his lips. Their kiss was sloppy, wet, urgent, filled with energy that zinged down Knight's spine. Their tongues dueled, and Day cupped the back of Knight's head, deepening the kiss, pausing only when they needed air.

Day's eyes shone as Knight looked deep into them before shifting back and taking Day in his mouth once again. The entire bed shook, not in great, flowing waves, but tiny shocks that rippled through the mattress and up Knight's legs, sending Day's desire into him. There were few things in the world sexier or hotter than being desired, and Day's eyes shone in a way that left Knight no doubt that he was desired, wanted—hell, he might have been needed. No one had needed him in a long time. That alone spurred Knight on, laving along Day's length, rolling his tongue around the base of Day's flared head, listening for any change in the chorus of moans that rapidly filled the room.

Knight could tell Day was getting close from the way he fisted the bedding, pulling it up from the sides, and his legs quivered under him. He figured Day was trying to prolong the sensation as long as possible, and Knight slowed his sucking, adding pressure but moving more languidly. He raised his gaze and saw Day had brought the heel of his hand to his mouth. Knight pulled it away, and Day groaned loudly, making sounds no person should make unless they were in the throes of uncontrolled passion.

He wanted to tell Day to let it go, but he sped up, adding more and more until Day gasped and went rigid, clamping his eyes closed before filling Knight's mouth with his release. Knight swallowed and sucked harder, taking all that Day had to give, and only after Day lay back on the bed, gasping for air, did he stop and let Day slip from his lips.

"You okay?" Knight asked as a smile formed on Day's lips and got bigger and brighter.

"Oh yeah. You blew my mind." Day whispered. "When I can move, I'll be happy to…." Day sighed and slowly rolled over, tugging Knight down on the bed. "You know, you're something else."

"I'm just me. A pain in the ass most of the time."

"Yeah, you are that. But you're my pain in the ass." Day swatted his butt lightly. "And under all those cactus prickles is a guy that I'm proud to have as a partner and one I know I'm pleased is in my life."

Knight noticed the way Day chose his words. "Are you trying not to freak me out?"

"Duh. I figure I can only expect you to take so many steps forward before your head explodes." Day latched onto his chest, sucking and licking while Knight lay back, arms spread wide, giving himself and his pleasure over to Day's loving hands and lips.

Knight clamped his eyes closed, realizing he'd let that word cross his mind in conjunction with Day. There was little doubt how he felt, or from his actions, how Day felt about him. Knight knew he'd have done anything to get Day back—ramming a car, taking a bullet, trading places with Day. As long as Day was safe, Knight had what he truly wanted.

"You know, you deserve so much better than me," Knight whispered. He felt Day still and without looking knew he was being stared at with the intensity of a laser beam. "You do. I'm a messed-up Marine who can't seem to figure out his own feelings without weeks of deliberation and circular thinking."

"Sometimes you're such an ass," Day said, but with no heat.

Knight couldn't read the tone and opened his eyes, just to see if the world had fallen off its axis. This was too good to be true, and he knew he wasn't dreaming, so some major catastrophe must have come to pass. Instead, Day's eyes shone as he looked at him. Knight wanted to know what that meant and what the hell he'd missed, but Day slid down him, took Knight's cock between his lips, and sucked like it was the end of the world. Conscious thought was impossible at that point. Hell, thinking of anything except Day was impossible, so he went with it, giving up the ruminations and half-assed soul-searching that had accompanied him for weeks. Maybe it was time for him to let it all go.

"Damn, you make me happy," Knight growled under his breath as Day took all of him deep, sucking like there was no tomorrow, short-circuiting his stubbornness.

"That's it, let it go," Day whispered, breaking his rhythm for a few seconds and then stealing Knight's breath once again.

Knight wiped his face as he tried to hold it together.

"Let it go," Day said again, and that tripped something inside.

Knight's passion erupted and he did as he was told, letting go of everything he'd been holding on to. He had no idea how long he lay there; all he knew was that Day was there with him, holding him as he had been for weeks. Through all his crap, Day had been there, and maybe it was time he opened up and truly let Day in. "When this is over and we get home where it's quiet and I can think, I'm going to tell you about Panama. All of it."

Day leaned upward, kissing him gently. He didn't say a thing, and when Knight opened his eyes after Day's lips pulled away, he saw understanding accompanied by a huge smile. It was time to talk, to bring all this out into the open; otherwise, it was going to eat him from the inside.

A sharp bang on the door made both of them jump. "If you're done scaring us straight people, I have something to eat. Come by in five minutes or there won't be anything left."

"Jesus Christ, if you'd told me that your brother had a mouth like yours on him, I probably would have left him lost." Knight groaned and waited for Day to get up and start dressing. He watched, sitting on the edge of the bed.

"Why do you think I didn't?" Day grinned as he pulled on his pants. "Get dressed before I jump you again."

"You can do that later—there's going to be plenty of time. They have us on ice until this whole thing goes down."

Day walked over and placed a hand on his cheek. "You grumble about the best things sometimes." He leaned down and kissed him.

Chapter 9

TWO DAYS. Day paced the room for the hundredth time that morning. He knew each stain in the carpet, each lump in the bed, and even the chips in the bathroom tile. Dimato had agreed with Royerston that they had done great work, but their visibility needed to fade away for a while, so they sat in the hotel and waited.

Knight wasn't faring much better. And Stephen? All he did was complain and rap on the wall whenever Day and Knight decided it was time to relieve a little boredom. Either they were loud or the walls in the hotel were paper-thin. Day had come to the conclusion that both were a possibility, but he didn't give a crap. Now that Knight seemed to have given up some of his reservations, the man was an animal, and Day was determined to get all he could before Knight rebuilt his walls. He had little doubt that Knight eventually would, but he was hopeful.

A knock on the door made Day tense. Knight opened it and Royerston strode inside—uniform, vest, loaded for bear.

"It's going down. We have word that Sanchez is in town, and he's been spotted." Royerston grinned. "You have to love men whose egos are so huge they actually believe they're untouchable."

"What did he do?" Day asked as Stephen joined them and shut the door.

"He rented the biggest limo in town. He was seen getting out of it at a restaurant downtown. We believed it was to meet with his associates, but he had dinner with a woman. They left in a hurry last night and have been holed up in a house. The limo has been returned, so he seems to understand he might have gone too far. Either that or someone else rented it for him. The thing is, we've been able to trace him and keep him under electronic surveillance. The captain is so thrilled that Sanchez is in our sights that he sent me over to ask if the three of you want in on the takedown."

"Yeah," Day said without hesitating. If he stayed in this room another minute, he was about to explode.

"Good. I have gear, but you have to stay out of the way. We're spread thin right now…."

Knight nodded. "So you want us to be your backup."

"Yeah. I want you to have my back."

"What about me?" Stephen asked.

"Homeland Security is in the loop, but we've all been careful. Men have flown in from DC and Los Angeles to help out. They asked if you'd join them. We need to get going. I hope you can gear up in the car." Royerston led the way out, and they climbed in the back of a huge SUV and took off.

"Jesus," Knight said, his eyes boggling like a kid in a candy store at the gear. They started putting it on as Royerston drove.

"Where are we going?" Day asked.

"Sanchez is staying at a rental house at the edge of town. He was smart there, and if it hadn't been for the limo and the information you guys provided, he never would have been on our radar."

Day pulled on the bulletproof vest and grabbed a helmet and the rest of the gear. His heart raced. "What do you want us to do?"

"You'll stay back and out of the way. The operation has been planned, and it should go off pretty well," Royerston said.

Knight turned to Day, and they shared a moment of crystal-clear communication. They were being brought in as sort of a consolation prize and that was about it. Of course, things could go wrong; they both knew it. But facts were facts.

Day shrugged and turned to look out the front window.

They pulled up to the police station and filed inside. Royerston led them to a room where a briefing was just ending. The Homeland Security guys folded Stephen into their ranks, and once again it was Day and Knight. It seemed they always ended up that way—the two of them against the world. Maybe that was how it was meant to be.

"We're going to head out in a matter of minutes," Day said.

"I hope like hell they have this figured correctly. This is a lot of planning and coordination to catch a man who could slip through their fingers in two seconds."

Day nodded his agreement and listened to the end of the briefing. Then they followed Royerston out of the station and back to the vehicle. "How do you know Sanchez hasn't already been tipped off?" Day asked Royerston as they drove.

"That's the shit part. We don't. Mostly we've tried to keep the people in the know to a minimum, but now we have to expand it to get the men we need."

Knight nodded, and Day could tell he was nervous. Most likely his Marine planning skills were kicking in and he could see the holes in what they were doing. Day hoped Royerston and his team caught a break.

"The house is a block away," Royerston said. The radio, which had been largely silent, burst to life as teams moved in around the house. Royerston took up a position out front while other units moved into positions around the back. They were well away from the house and watched as officers went to neighbors, knocking and presumably making sure they were safe and instructing them to take cover.

The call was made, announcing who they were and telling Sanchez to come out. At first there was no response, but when they received an answer, it was with bullets. Day got down and tugged Knight along with him. Fire was exchanged, and at least two cries went up from inside the house. Then it grew quiet.

"Come out with your hands up!" someone said over a bullhorn.

Stephen hurried over, crouched low. "This is too easy," he whispered. "Sanchez wouldn't give up without taking as many people with him as possible."

"Maybe he's already dead," Knight suggested, but something inside Day wasn't buying it.

He moved farther away down the street, looking at the other yards. "That place looks like it's been empty for a while," Day said, pointing to the house next door. They knocked on the door, but no one answered.

"So?" Stephen said.

Knight smacked Stephen's shoulder. "He has good instincts," Knight said and turned to Day. "What are you thinking?"

Day didn't answer. "Come on," he said and took off away from the others to the empty house. The backyard had a high fence, and the view of the yard from the neighboring house was obstructed. Day reached the fence and pulled open the gate, with Stephen staying behind to cover it. He kept low, knowing Knight was right behind him. A small shed sat near the fence, and Day used it as cover as he looked around the yard.

"What are you thinking?" Knight breathed just loudly enough for Day to hear.

"He's going to have an escape route of some kind."

At that moment, shooting started in the front of the house. Knight tensed, and Day leaned forward, watching.

Within about thirty seconds, two men from the neighboring yard crawled through a small hole in the fence, crouching as they raced across the yard toward the back door of the empty house.

"Don't move," Knight called, turning his gun on them.

The younger of the two men whipped around. Day's finger tightened on the trigger of his gun, but Knight shot first, taking the man down. The older man made a run for the house.

"Don't try it, Mr. Sanchez," Day said. "I'll shoot you, and believe me, I'll make it very painful."

Sanchez stopped, raising his hands. Day hadn't been sure what he'd expected—maybe someone younger, more vital. But Sanchez looked more like a middle-aged businessman than a criminal ringleader. He even wore a tie, his shirt open at the collar. The shooting out front died away, obviously a diversion.

"Lie down on the ground, hands flat," Day said.

"I can make things worth your while," Sanchez said as he looked toward the back door. "I have people and money to give you a life you could only dream of."

Day stepped closer, keeping a bead on him while Knight secured his arms and checked his pockets. They hadn't been issued cuffs, but Day found some old clothesline cord on the ground and tossed it to Knight, who tied Sanchez's hands.

"I don't think so," Day said to Sanchez. "See, I don't dream of money, but I'd love to see a world where people like you can't ruin other people's lives. And today, right now—" Day knelt down to look Sanchez right in his shit-brown eyes. "—I got a little closer to my dream."

"What are you two doing back here?" Royerston asked as he hurried into the yard. "One of the officers said you had come this way, and…." He stopped when he saw the man on the ground.

"Royerston, I'd like you to meet Carlos Sanchez. Doesn't look so powerful now, does he?"

Royerston's mouth worked, but nothing came out.

"It seems the shooting from the front was a diversion so he could get out the side, using his little escape plan." Day stood, still watching Sanchez. "He offered everything we could possibly want if we let him go. So you be sure to add attempted bribery to what is sure to be a monumental list of charges."

"We certainly will," Royerston said before speaking into the radio. Within seconds other officers joined them, and Sanchez was unceremoniously lifted to his feet and half dragged away. "All right. You're going to need to explain how you did that."

"It was Day," Knight said, turning to him. "He saw that the house seemed empty."

"I just thought that I'd have an escape plan if I were him, and since this house was empty, I headed over. I suspect he was going to get inside and then either wait it out or try to get another house away. It wouldn't take long for him to get some distance once he slipped the net here."

"But how did you see what he was doing?" Royerston asked.

"My partner is that good. He sees what others don't," Knight explained. "It's part of what makes him so good." Knight smiled, and Day nodded but said nothing, his mind still on the way Knight had said the word partner, as though it meant more than its context. "I suggest you have someone trail that back and see where he came from." Knight indicated the hole in the fence.

"We're securing the house now, but it's going to take a while." Royerston led the way out of the yard and back around to the front, where Captain Jacobs was frantically issuing orders. "Captain," Royerston said, pointing. "It seems our friends headed him off."

Relief flooded the captain's eyes.

"He was trying to get across the neighboring property."

"Why wasn't that already secured?" Jacobs barked at no one in particular. Day figured it was bluster and relief. "We've rounded up the rest and are cleaning out the house. We have at least two dead and one officer down."

"And Sanchez in custody," Royerston added with a smile.

"Yes." Captain Jacobs turned to Day. "It seems we have you to thank for saving our asses."

Day shook his head. "It was all of us working together. I'm glad I could be part of the team."

Captain Jacobs stared at him for two seconds. "Young man, you are so full of shit." Then he broke into a smile. "We got him." Jacobs hurried off, most likely to take custody of the prisoner and probably to make sure that any media pictures taken included him.

Not that Day cared in the least. He'd done what he'd come here to do. Stephen had been in trouble, and now he was safe and whole.

"Did you get to cuff him?" Day asked Stephen.

"Yeah. They gave me that honor," Stephen said grinning.

Day knew the satisfaction of successfully completing an assignment, and he was glad he could share this kind of moment with his brother. They hadn't been able to spend nearly enough time together, and Day missed it.

"Christmas is in about ten days. I was wondering if the two of you were going to stay," Stephen said, turning to Day. "We could have it at my house—the big one, that is—before I sell it. There's plenty of room."

Day looked at Knight and then back at his brother. "We have to get home and back to the office. But why don't you fly out to see us?"

"We can get together at my house if you like," Knight said. "I have room."

Day took a step back. He knew that was a big step for Knight. They hadn't talked about holidays other than once, when Knight told him he didn't celebrate them any longer and then had gotten that look like he desperately wanted a drink.

"All right, guys, let's wrap it up here," Captain Jacobs called over the din and then approached them. "I don't know how to thank you boys. You made the Phoenix PD look like national heroes and did the heavy work bringing down one of the men who has been running crime in this area for decades."

"You just tell my boss that. He'll be happy and maybe he'll get off Knight's back for a while." Day leaned closer. "I have no idea what's between them, but I swear one day they're going to grab rulers."

Jacobs threw his head back and laughed. "Damn, I'd like to see that. Well… maybe not." He hurried off, and Royerston led them back to the SUV.

"Where do you want me to drop you?" he asked.

"Take us to the hotel so we can get our things," Knight said. "Then do you think you could drop us at a hotel near the airport? We need to make some arrangements, and then we can get out of your hair." Knight turned to Day. "I'd like to stay here a few more days. I'm not looking forward to going back to snow, but Dimato will have a fit if we don't get back to work."

"It's all right." Day turned to Stephen. "Are you coming with us?"

"No. I have my own mopping up to do. We have some house cleaning to take care of. Border Patrol is going to need all the help they can get. Call me and let me know where you're staying, and we'll have a real nice dinner before you leave." Stephen pulled him into his arms, hugging Day hard. "I can't tell you how proud I am of you."

"Hey… that goes both ways."

"Well, you did great, and I'm sure I can get the time off to come see you, even if I'll freeze my nuts off the entire time." Stephen released him and stepped back. He and Knight shared a handshake. "You take care of each other." Stephen hurried away, and Day and Knight got in the back of the SUV.

Royerston wove through the cars and drove them back to the hotel, where they gathered what they had before taking them to a hotel by the airport.

"It's been real interesting to meet you," Royerston said once he'd pulled up under the canopy. "The next time you're coming to town, you be sure to call so I'll know when to take my vacation." He grinned and shook hands with both of them. "You two have guts, I have to give you that."

"Thanks. If you're in our neck of the woods, let us know and we'll show you some excitement, Yankee-style," Day teased, and then they went into the hotel. He was so glad this was over and his family was whole once again.

"You going to be able to take your brother being just as much of an adrenaline junkie as you are?" Knight asked with a sigh as he flopped down on the white, crisp-sheeted hotel bed. "I think I'm going to sleep for three days when I get home. I'm sick of hotel beds and want my own."

"Speaking of that, I'm going to shower while you call Dimato and arrange for a flight home." He figured he'd give Knight that chore and heard the grousing begin but stop when he closed the bathroom door. Day got undressed and started the water, then got under the spray. He closed his eyes and let the tension roll off him. He'd had enough chasing and shooting for a while.

"We have a flight home tomorrow," Knight said as he came into the bathroom. Day expected him to leave, but Knight pulled the shower curtain aside and stepped in with him. As soon as he pulled the curtain closed, Knight pressed up against Day's back, arms encircling him, sliding his hands over Day's chest, circling one of his nipples with one finger.

Day groaned and let go of the last of the worry he'd been carrying. Now *this* kind of stress relief he could do for hours.

THEIR FLIGHT the following morning was at some ungodly hour, and Day slept for most of it. By the time they landed, changed planes, and then arrived in Milwaukee, Day was still wiped out. Sleep or not, plane travel sucked.

"I could sleep for a week," Knight said once they were finally on the road away from the airport. "I hate to admit it, but I'm not as young as I used to be, and those days in the desert really took it out of me."

Day said nothing. He didn't remind Knight that the time they had been in the desert was nearly a week earlier, or that they'd had plenty of downtime. "It has nothing to do with getting older and more to do with growing up. Stuff like that is fine, but nothing beats heating, air-conditioning, and a bed that isn't sand with the occasional bug thrown in for good measure."

"Amen to that," Knight agreed as he pulled up in front of Day's apartment. "I was wondering if you'd like to come over tomorrow. I haven't decorated for the holidays since…. Well, in a while, and I thought maybe you could help me. If your brother is going to visit, he deserves better than a bare house."

Day turned in the seat. "Are you sure about that?" He knew this was one of those moments of decision. If Knight wanted an out, Day would give it to him.

Knight nodded. "Yeah. I think it's about time… for a lot of things." Then Knight reached out, slid his hand around the back of Day's neck, and pulled him in for a kiss.

Stay tuned for an
excerpt from

Day and Knight

Day and Knight: Book 1

By Dirk Greyson

    As former NSA, Dayton (Day) Ingram has national security chops and now works as a technical analyst for Scorpion. He longs for fieldwork, and scuttling an attack gives him his chance. He's smart, multilingual, and a technological wizard. But his opportunity comes with a hitch—a partner, Knighton (Knight), who is a real mystery. Despite countless hours of research, Day can find nothing on the agent, including his first name!

    Former Marine Knight crawled into a bottle after losing his family. After drying out, he's offered one last chance: along with Day, stop a terrorist threat from the Yucatan. To get there without drawing suspicion, Day and Knight board a gay cruise, where the deeply closeted Day and equally closeted Knight must pose as a couple. Tensions run high as Knight communicates very little and Day bristles at Knight's heavy-handed need for control.

    But after drinking too much, Day and Knight wake up in bed. *Together*. As they near their destination, they must learn to trust and rely on each other to infiltrate the terrorist camp and neutralize the plot aimed at the US's technological infrastructure, if they hope to have a life after the mission. One that might include each other.

www.dreamspinnerpress.com

Chapter 1

DAYTON INGRAM had never thought of this area of Milwaukee as particularly dangerous. The restaurants and businesses on Mitchell Street were bustling with customers, but two blocks made a real difference. He should have waited to find a parking space closer to the Wild Chili, but it had been light out when he arrived at the restaurant, and now that darkness had fallen, the welcoming feeling faded as he walked into a neighborhood he wasn't familiar with. Dayton picked up the pace and began walking faster toward his Ford Fusion. He'd was just approaching it when a cry reached his ears. He stopped, listening intently the way he'd been taught, to pick up the direction, hoping he would hear it again.

It came again, louder this time and much more frantic. "I have done nothing to you," a young voice pleaded in Spanish. "Leave me alone."

The reply came, also in Spanish, menacing, growly. "Why should we?"

Instantly Day headed in that direction. He reached for his phone and pulled it from his pocket. He pressed the button to wake it up, and it remained dark.

"Shit!" he swore, kicking himself for not checking it earlier. He'd felt it vibrate a few times during dinner but had figured it was Facebook or something like that. Instead the damn thing had been telling him it was almost out of power. He needed to see about getting a new battery for the piece of shit—he'd charged the fucking thing just before he'd left the house.

"Leave me alone." The cry repeated, this time in distress and accompanied by the sounds of a scuffle and an overturned trash can rumbling on concrete as it went. Day took off in the direction of the sound, rounding the corner of a small alley that stank of garbage and God knew what else, where two heavyset men in ratty sweatshirts and stained pants hanging halfway down to their knees loomed over a teenager, or someone not much older than that.

"Just give us your money, and we'll let you be, *maricón*," the man spat, puffing up his chest in a display of machismo. "Otherwise we'll cut your balls off." The man held up his hand, a knife flashed, and Day stopped a few feet away, just out of arm's reach.

"*Huye!*" he cried at the top of his lungs to the kid. "Get out of here," he added as the men advanced on him. Dayton kept his cool and widened his stance, carefully watching the glazed eyes of both men. The one with the knife came first, jabbing it at him a little clumsily. Dayton danced back out of his reach and waited for another pass. It looked like the fat man's friend was going to see what happened before he entered the fray. Stupid mistake. They might have been able to get to him if they worked together—might. But alone, no way in hell!

"It's two against one, gringo," the man warned, and Dayton caught a hint of alcohol on his breath. "Give us your money too, and we'll let you live." He swung the knife, and Dayton caught his arm before it reached the apex of the arc. Holding the man's hand firmly in his, he twisted around and flipped him over his shoulder. The knife flew out of the assailant's hand, clattering to the concrete, and he landed on his back with a hard thud and didn't move. Day swung around to the other man, ready for his attack, but none came.

He expected the man to flee, but whatever he was on must have made him brave and too stupid to know better. He'd grabbed the kid and was holding him as a shield. "Stay still," Dayton said and locked gazes with the man. His eyes were wide, and Dayton guessed he'd been drinking, at least, and maybe had taken a hit of something else. As he took a step closer, not looking away, the man's eyes widened enough that they caught the light. His pupils were huge. Yeah, he was definitely high.

Dayton breathed evenly, remembering his training, pushing aside the nerves that threatened to cloud his concentration. What he'd been taught and practiced had worked once already. He did his best to keep his racing heart from pounding too loudly in his ears.

"Back up, gringo."

"Let the kid go, and you can leave," Dayton said levelly, even as he was starting to wonder if this whole situation was getting out of control. He'd meant to help the kid, not make things worse.

"Instead I maybe break his neck," the man said, smiling to show a mouth full of rotten teeth.

Dayton crouched slightly, and when the man's gaze shifted to the kid, Dayton took a step forward. He swept his leg out in a kick that caught the mugger's leg. The man lost his balance, falling to the ground. Dayton was ready in case the kid fell too, but he managed to jump away. "Call the police," Dayton ordered, and the kid nodded, pulling a phone out of his pocket while Dayton grabbed the man, rolled him over, and held his hands. "Give me your belt."

"What for?" the kid asked but then opened his belt and handed it over. Dayton used it to fasten the man's hands behind him. The other one groaned, and Dayton warned him not to move unless he wanted more. He thought he heard the man mutter, "*No más.*"

Sirens sounded, and Day looked around. "Are you okay, kid?" He nodded. "I have to go. Tell them what happened, and the police will see to it that these two are taken care of."

"You're leaving? You saved my life," the kid said in English as he continued shaking a little.

"I'm glad I could help," Dayton said with a smile. Then he turned and walked calmly down the street, got in his car, and drove slowly off as police vehicles began to arrive behind him. As he drove, Day plugged in his phone, got the beginning of a charge, and called in to the office.

"I need to speak to Gladstone," Day said when the call was answered and then waited to be transferred. He steered his car onto the freeway as his boss answered. Day switched the phone to hands-free as he sped up. "Remember you said to tell you if anything unusual happened...," Dayton began and then relayed the incident.

"Did the police see you?"

"No. I left before they got there," Dayton answered.

"Okay. We'll take care of it, but come into my office first thing in the morning." The call ended abruptly, and Dayton hung up and drove the rest of the way to his South-Side home.

He pulled up to the house, sliding past it before turning down the alley. He parked his car in the garage that he paid a little extra to use and then walked to the house. He unlocked his ground-floor door and then took the stairs up to the second floor of the duplex. It was a nice place—compact and affordable. Once inside he closed the main door and walked back to the bedroom. He set his keys in their place on the dresser, along with his wallet. Then he plugged in his phone and arranged it in its place next to his wallet. Finally, he took off his shoes, filling in the space they'd left on the floor of his closet, then left the room and returned to his living room.

He sat on the serviceable but old sofa he'd found at a thrift store and covered with a slipcover to make it look less hideous. He'd done the same thing with the two chairs. They were comfortable enough, and that was all that mattered to him. He made do, and there was something familiar and almost homey about it. The same could be said of the mismatched chairs pushed into place around the table in his small dining room. And no one would know how old and scarred the tabletop was unless they lifted the sapphire tablecloth to peer under it.

Day turned on the television and did his best to relax, but the incident in the alley kept running through his mind. He'd been trying to help, and in the end he had, but he'd also put the kid in more danger, if momentarily. His boss hadn't said anything about whether he thought Dayton had done the right thing. Well, it was too late now, and if he'd screwed up with his rashness, so be it. He'd helped the kid and had gotten him away from the men.

Laughter came from the television, pulling him out of his thoughts for a little while. He turned his attention to the rerun of *Will and Grace*, laughing a few times before changing the channel once the show was over. He settled on an episode of *The Mentalist*. It was an unrealistic portrayal, but it was entertaining. Secretly, however, he wanted to be just like Patrick Jane—keenly observant, a student of human nature—and have the ability to get in other people's heads. After watching the episode, he turned off the television.

The tiny second bedroom in the apartment acted as Dayton's office. Before going to bed, he sat at his desk, started up his laptop, and checked his personal e-mail. It was mostly junk, but there was a note from his brother about his latest lame scheme to make himself a pile of money so he could continue his wandering lifestyle forever. Like all the other "opportunities," Stephen made it sound as though it were the deal of the century, but Dayton could see the holes in it a mile away and shook his head. He should call him, but he wasn't in the mood to have that conversation tonight. So after checking the last of his e-mail, he closed the computer lid and headed to the bathroom, where he cleaned up and got ready for bed.

THE FOLLOWING morning, pressed and dressed, he left his apartment and drove to a brick office building that had once housed a bank. It still looked like a bank, which was probably why it worked so well for its new purpose. The sign out front read "S L S Inc." It stood for Scorpion Logistics Services. But everyone inside knew those words meant something very different than the public might take them to mean. People asked him if they were a trucking and shipment management company, and Dayton always answered yes but was vague about what he did.

He parked in his space alongside the building and pulled his badge out of his wallet. He scanned it at the door reader, and it clicked. He pulled the door open and entered the building. He scanned his card at the next door and placed his thumb on the pad. When the door clicked open, he walked farther into the building.

"Good morning," the receptionist said professionally, barely looking up from her keyboard as she typed.

Dayton knew she wasn't being rude, just efficient, and he returned her greeting before continuing on to his cubicle. He sat down and started up his computer, entered himself into the system, and checked the programs he'd set to run overnight. They had finished, and he smiled before picking up the phone.

"Gladstone."

Jason Gladstone. Everyone just called him Gladstone, and a few people dared to call him Glad, but Dayton never had and doubted he ever would.

"You wanted to see me this morning?" Dayton said.

"Uh… yeah. Come to my office in an hour. Uh… good morning." He hung up, and Dayton placed his phone back in its place. His boss was a weird duck. Smart as they came, but social niceties tended to get lost in his intensity. Not that Dayton minded. He went back to work analyzing the data he'd collected, and then, once he'd finished the report, he sent it off to the requestor. He saved the information in case it needed to be reworked but set it for auto-purge in a month. Then he went to Gladstone's office.

"Dayton," Gladstone said after he knocked on the doorframe. "Come with me."

He stood slowly and nodded, following his boss through the building and into one of the small conference rooms. Gladstone closed the door and motioned Dayton to take a seat while he sat just opposite him. Fuck, he was in trouble. That was the only explanation.

"We got some additional information on the incident last night from the police. Apparently you left out some details when we talked last night." Gladstone stared at him intently.

"I believe I told you everything."

Gladstone smacked a file onto the table and slid it over to him. Dayton glanced down at it and saw it had his name on it. "You never told any of us that you speak Spanish."

Huh? Dayton covered his confusion. Even in the office, he'd learned to maintain a façade of strength and unflappability. "It's a new skill. I decided to learn about a year ago, and I've been practicing with a number of people conversationally online. I was surprised at how quickly I could pick it up." He didn't smile, even though he was fucking proud of himself. He spoke a number of other languages as well, so he did have a gift for them.

Gladstone pulled the file back and opened it. "You were hired away from the NSA six months ago, and the reason you gave for wanting to join us was that you wanted to do fieldwork, and that wasn't going to happen there. Well, up until last night, no one thought you had what it took for fieldwork, but you've changed some minds." Gladstone didn't look happy. "And your newly acquired skill seems to have sealed the deal."

"All right. Do you have a new project for me?" Dayton kept his excitement out of his voice. He loved gathering and analyzing data, especially when there was an external challenge involved.

"Don't know yet. A team is being assembled, and you're on the short list for consideration. Doesn't mean you'll be chosen, but the powers that be are moving quickly on this, so be ready to go, and make sure your affairs are in order to be away from home for a period of time."

"How long would I be away?" Dayton asked.

"That wasn't shared with me," Gladstone answered flatly. "But they were also interested in your more clandestine computer skills as well as… your looks." Gladstone's possum-like eyes bored into him.

Dayton didn't flinch. Gladstone was never going to win any beauty contests. He'd been in the clandestine-operations business for quite a while and knew his way around, but the man had most definitely been hired for his skills.

"My looks?" Dayton asked. That seemed the most unlikely of all his traits to have garnered him consideration for a field operation. "I work hard, and I'm fucking good at what I do." His hackles raised in a split second.

"Cool down, Ingram. I wasn't casting aspersions on your qualifications, just stating facts." Gladstone's expression softened slightly.

"So what do I do now?" He really wanted to get into fieldwork.

"Nothing. If you're chosen you'll be contacted, and they'll arrange to meet and brief you. That division of the organization is as secretive and closemouthed as they get. They tell no one anything they don't need to know, and that even goes for me." Gladstone paused. "You're here in part because of your skills, and in part because you know how to keep your mouth shut. There may be training involved, but I don't know for sure." He stood up, a signal that the meeting was over. "Just be prepared to pick up and go at a moment's notice." Gladstone picked up the file and left the room, closing the door behind him.

Dayton wanted to crow to the rooftops. He was actually being considered for fieldwork. How fucking awesome was that? Of course, he kept his cool and left the room a minute after Gladstone, his expression schooled and his walk as normal as he could make it. He went back to his desk and got to work.

"What did the Weeble want?" Kyper Morris asked, popping his head over the cubicle. How Kyper had gotten his job, Dayton didn't know. He was gossipy and tended to talk. A lot. Granted, Dayton never heard him say anything he shouldn't, but how he could talk so damned much and not accidentally spill something he shouldn't was beyond Dayton. "Did you do something? I heard there was an incident last night."

Just like any office, there was a rumor mill here as well, but it tended to be quite subdued. "He wanted to talk," Dayton answered.

"You're no fun," Kyper said, and Dayton heard the chair squeak, which meant Kyper had plopped himself onto his chair in a show of disappointment. "You know, we all took this job because of the potential excitement, and what do we see? The same four walls and reams of data. We might as well be working at Walmart." The clicking of keys was nearly deafening. When Kyper got pissed about something, he typed as hard as hell.

"Give it a rest," Dayton called as lightly as he could. The pounding eased off, but the typing continued. Dayton went back to work, searching for the data locations he could use to put together the analysis request he'd just been sent.

"So, was it good news?" Kyper asked a few minutes later. The man was like a dog with a bone—he never let anything go. Dayton ignored him and continued working. It hadn't worked before, and it wasn't likely to work now. Kyper's special skill was that he never gave up. If there was a way to get something he needed, he would stop at nothing until he had it in hand. The only time he'd ever given up on anything was when Gladstone had threatened his ability to have children. Even then, he'd only backed off, and a few days later he was crowing about solving the problem.

Dayton took a break and got a cup of coffee from the snack area. He brought it back to his desk and settled in to work for the rest of the morning. He left for lunch and returned with takeout that he ate at his desk. When he was done, he wadded up the paper and tossed it into the trash.

"Two points."

Dayton turned around and shivered as a man with a pair of black, almost hollow eyes stared right back and through him. It was the coldest gaze he'd ever seen in his life. "Dimato," the man said with no emotion whatsoever. Dayton knew instantly that it wasn't his real name.

"Ingram," he said, standing up and offering his hand.

The man stood there and did nothing. "Come with me."

Dayton lowered his hand and followed Dimato out of the cubicle area and up the stairs. They passed through various secure areas, with Dimato getting them access.

They entered an office, and Dimato closed the door. "All right," he began, pointing to a chair. Dayton sat, and Dimato pulled another from around the polished conference table and lowered himself into it, getting comfortable. "As you've been told, we have been looking at you for an assignment." Dayton had expected him to have a file or some information, but he simply sat and watched him. Dayton forced himself not to squirm. Dimato's attitude was designed to make him uncomfortable, but he'd be damned if these kinds of games would have an effect on him, so he waited, refusing to break eye contact.

"Yes. I was told nothing other than it would require me to be away for a period of time."

Dimato nodded. "We have a situation, and we need someone with your particular blend of skills."

"And what would that be?" Dayton pressed, leaning forward.

"Your computer skills are top-notch, you speak multiple languages, including Spanish, which tipped the decision in your favor, and frankly, your appearance was a plus as well." He crossed one leg over the other. "We do have concerns, one being your lack of fieldwork. But we were all new once, and you have good instincts. The other is… harder to explain. In the field you must put the mission and the safety of the team above everything else. Last night, according to the information gathered, you were cool under pressure and saved the kid. But by getting involved, you put yourself in unnecessary danger. In the field, choosing your battles can mean the difference between success and failure. This isn't a game. It's dangerous." Those emotionless black eyes were making Dayton's skin crawl.

"I understand that." He'd always known what was required. "When will I meet the others I'll work with? I'm assuming I won't be sent in alone."

"I'm expecting him at any time," Dimato said. He didn't move, but his gaze did shift slightly. Dayton had noticed a set of world clocks on the wall when he'd come in, so Dimato was checking the time.

"He's late," Dayton said flatly. Dimato didn't react, other than a slight twitch of his lips. The office door opened. Dayton turned in his chair as an older man stepped in and closed the door.

"This is Knighton from Records and Research," Dimato said. "He'll be your partner on this particular assignment."

"Him?" Dayton asked, eyes widening. That was hard to believe. He seemed a little old, with gray hair at the temples and a slight slouch to his posture. He seemed a little like he'd been rode hard and put away wet. Granted, he was handsome enough, with a strong, chiseled jaw covered with stubble that looked like he hadn't bothered to shave as opposed to a fashion choice, and piercing eyes that Dayton doubted missed much.

"Yes, me," Knighton said firmly in a rich baritone. He sat down at the chair across from Dayton and made himself comfortable. "What's the deal, so I can decide if I want to take it?" He leaned back in his chair, hands behind his head.

Dimato stood up and walked to where Knighton sat. He braced his arms on the edge of the table and leaned over it. "This is your final chance for fieldwork." So there was emotion Dimato somewhere. "You've buried yourself in the research department for almost two years, and it's time you either shit or got off the pot."

Dayton wasn't sure he should be here for this. He swallowed hard and turned away. But like a train wreck, it was hard not to watch.

"This requires your skills, and we need you. So get over yourself and get back on the horse. Once this is over, you can go back to research for the rest of your life for all I care."

Dayton turned slightly. Knighton's expression hadn't changed, except his lips curled up into a slight smile, making Dayton wonder if this was all some act for his benefit. He didn't see what the motivation could possibly be, but it seemed to him this sort of conversation should have been held behind closed doors.

"Since you asked so nicely…," Knighton began.

Dimato moved back to his seat as though nothing had happened.

Dayton acted the same way and turned toward the man he assumed was his boss now.

"One of our departments picked up some chatter coming out of Mexico. We get it all the time and turn most of what we suspect over to the DEA, but this is different and doesn't seem to be drug-related. It's centering on an attack of some type on the electronic intelligence infrastructure here in the US." Dimato stood and retrieved two folders from his desk. He handed one to each of them. "These are to be destroyed if you are in danger or compromised in any way."

"Understood," Dayton said as he took the file with a slight tremor of excitement in his hand. "May I ask why the CIA isn't involved?"

"We brought it to their attention, and they, in their infinite wisdom, punted it back to us, claiming budget cuts. The truth is they don't see this as the threat we know it is." Dimato shook his head. "So we're sending you in to neutralize it. We believe—and the details of what we have are in the folder—that they plan to make this attack in the next two weeks."

"When you say electronic infrastructure, you mean the Internet, correct?" Knighton asked.

"Yes."

"But isn't there security already? Websites have security and so do their back-end systems. It isn't flawless, but how can someone attack that when it's so dispersed?"

Dayton gasped and looked at Dimato, but he just sat quietly.

"That's easy. Any security system can be gotten around. It's a multibillion-dollar business," Dayton said to Knighton. "Hackers and threats get more and more sophisticated each year, and so do the security precautions that guard against them. It's a never-ending cycle." Dayton then turned to Dimato. "There are a number of systemic holes that could be exploited. Some I suspect have been anticipated but others probably haven't. The terrorists may have hit on some as yet undiscovered hole and are working on a way to exploit it."

"Could you do that? Exploit a security hole?" Dimato asked.

Dayton smiled. "I do it every day. That's how I get some of the critical data we need. We don't use it for nefarious purposes, and I schedule it all for deletion once we are through with it, but if I can do it, so can others. Do we know the exact threat?"

"No," Dimato said. "That's part of the problem. Gentlemen, we need you to determine the source of the threat. It's originating in the Yucatan Peninsula of Mexico, and we believe it's near the border with Belize. That area is sparsely populated, with plenty of remote areas where a plot like this could be hatched and carried out. The team here will supply support, but we need boots on the ground, and that's you two."

"How are we getting there? By plane?" Knighton asked.

"No. We need to make sure you slip into the area under the radar. If this group, and that's our assumption, is savvy enough to do this, then a plane or anything out of the ordinary would be spotted."

"We could fly over at night, and you could drop us out of the plane. We'd hit the ground, ditch the chutes, and no one would be the wiser. That area is dark as shit at night." For the first time, Knighton seemed really engaged.

"We can't take the chance. We'll only get one shot at this. If we blow it, they'll move, and we will have to start all over again. The team is still trying to figure out how to get you in with no one noticing."

"How about a cruise ship?" Dayton suggested. "You said this is near the border with Belize. There are cruise ships that stop in Costa Maya, which is in that area. A friend took one last year. They run Sunday to Sunday. I think she left out of Fort Lauderdale. We could arrive on the ship in Costa Maya. No one would be looking for us in a group of tourists. We simply book an excursion inland and then disappear. When we don't return, the ship will sail on without us."

"Aren't ships like that booked?" Knighton asked.

Dayton shrugged, but Dimato was already out of his chair and picking up his phone. "Research cruises leaving this weekend from any port, docking in Costa Maya, Mexico, and arrange for a cabin. If they're full you'll need to arrange for existing passengers to be waylaid or shifted off the cruise. Everything must be done not to raise suspicion." He hung up and sat back down. "We'll arrange for both of you to have access to the transmissions we've intercepted."

"Excellent, sir," Dayton said. He was anxious to see what they were getting into and to look for clues about this mysterious threat.

No one said anything more, and Dayton wondered if the meeting was over. He waited for Dimato to stand and then did the same. Dayton stepped toward the door, with Knighton remaining behind.

"By the way," Dimato said. "Your desk and things have been relocated to this floor. See Eileen just outside. She'll show you where it is and give you a new badge and explain the security requirements to get on this floor. It's good to have you on the team."

Dayton pulled the door open, stunned, and stepped outside, where Eileen was waiting for him. The middle-aged woman screamed efficiency, from the tailored way she was dressed, down to her highly polished, sensible shoes. She led him briskly toward what appeared to be an office. There were two desks inside. "This space will be for you and Knight. We find that operational teams need to be kept together so information can be shared in a secure environment." She stepped inside and directed him toward the desk closest to the window. "We set up your things there. Here's your new badge." She took the old one and bent it in half. "I'll have this shredded. You won't need it any longer."

"Will I be restricted from any parts of the building?"

"Only the computer operations center. Everything else will be open to you. If you need something and you aren't getting cooperation, let me or Dimato know, and we'll take care of it." She paused. "Is there anything else I can do for you?" She obviously didn't anticipate anything because she was already turning to leave the room. She closed the door, and it took all Dayton's self-control not to jump up and pound his fist in the air. Instead, he booted up his computer to clear the work he'd left undone and then opened the file folder he'd been given and began to read.

AN HOUR or so later, the door bounced open. He jumped and then looked up, and Knighton walked in, surveying the space as though he owned it.

"I see you already took the desk near the window."

Dayton was about to argue and say that his things had been put there for him, but he kept quiet and returned his attention to the file.

"You aren't going to find much in there other than the standard information and a little more detail about what we've already been told," Knight said. A folded piece of paper landed on Dayton's desk.

Dayton ignored it for the time being. "Do you always enter a room like a herd of elephants? I understand we all have skills. Is that listed among yours?" He raised his eyebrows and then went back to the file. He was nearly done and wanted to make sure he had all of the information in his brain before he went to work on the messages that had been intercepted. A series of encrypted files from Eileen had been waiting on his computer in his new office. He'd only glanced at them and realized he needed the background information before he could dig into the transmissions themselves.

"Look, kid, I have years of experience at this sort of thing. So let me do what I do best, and you can do the computer stuff, and maybe we'll get out of this alive and back home so we can go on with our lives." Knight dropped the file on his desk and schlumped into his chair.

"If you don't want to do this, then tell them instead of acting like a grumpy old man," Dayton countered. Then he sighed. This was not the way to start what should be a partnership. "Let's start over rather than snapping at each other. I'm Dayton Ingram. My friends call me Day." He walked over to the other desk and extended his hand.

The other man stared at it for a second, and then he stood as well. "Knighton. People call me Knight."

"Is that your first or last name?" Day said as he shook the offered hand.

"Just Knighton," he said, and then he dropped the hand. "So did you find any pearl of wisdom in there?"

"Not really, just background information. But some of it might be helpful." He returned to his computer, opened one of the encrypted files Eileen had sent, and turned the monitor so Knight could see it. "The signals they intercepted have been traced to this area, here. But according to what's in the file, it isn't coming from the same place each time."

"So they're moving around. That's going to make it more difficult to find," Knight commented as he walked over to Day's desk.

"That's a possibility, but it could also be that there's something distorting the signal."

"Like what?"

"I don't know. But we'll get some answers when we get there. There are a number of reasons why the signal could be distorted or intermittent." Day made a note on a pad on the desk. "I'll research and see what I can find."

"Good," Knight said. Thankfully this time no attitude accompanied it. "Are you going to see what you can make of the transmissions?"

"Yes," Day answered, already pulling up the files after turning his monitor around. Knight walked toward the door. "What are you going to do?"

"Travel arrangements." Knight pulled open the door and closed it after he left. Day watched him go, wondering what in hell he had gotten himself into. Knight was handsome enough—Whoa, he needed to stop right there. He'd be working with Knight for weeks, and anyway, he had no intention of putting one single toe outside the proverbial closet, not while what he wanted was within his grasp. He'd kept his sexual orientation to himself for a long time. The last time he'd ventured out, things had not gone well at all. He would keep his interest, whatever the hell that was, to himself.

Dayton glanced at the paper Knight had plopped on his desk. It was some basic information about travel expenses. He knew what to do; he wasn't dumb. Shaking his head, he returned to his computer and went to work on the messages to see if there was anything he could learn. He spent much of the rest of the day on them, doing his level best to ignore Knight's comings and goings in the office.

"Are you going to knock off for the night or sleep at your desk, newbie?" Knight asked, breaking Day's concentration. "I have our travel arrangements all set, and the company even sprang for a decent stateroom."

"We're only going to be on the ship a few days. It seems like a waste to—"

Knight cut him off with a wave of his hand. "You've been busy and haven't heard the latest. The sailing we're on is a gay cruise, so you and I are playing the part of lovers on a vacation together."

Day's stomach did a flip, and he tried his best to keep his discomfort off his face. "Sounds… interesting." God, what in the hell did he say to that?

"Don't worry, we don't have to take it too far, but it was the easiest way to get us on the ship we need, and it will help us blend in with the other passengers." Knight handed him a set of papers. "Put this someplace safe. That should be all your travel arrangements."

Day nodded, reading through the details.

"I'll see you tomorrow," Knight said. "And you're welcome."

Day looked up from the travel documents and opened his mouth to say thank you, but Knight was already leaving the office with the grace of a panther on the prowl. Day was transfixed, his mind instantly stripping away the dress shirt and pants, imagining what might be hidden beneath. Probably acres of rich olive-toned skin with just enough short dark hair on his chest to make things really interesting. Day's mind conjured up a scent that made his head swim.

"Practicing for the cruise?" Knight asked from the doorway, and Day blinked once as he fell back to reality.

"Just wondering if being an ass came naturally to you or if you actually worked at it?" Day flashed a smile, thankful he'd been able to come up with something to cover his little daydream. Shit like that had to end. He needed to keep things together. He could do this.

"It's a talent gifted by the gods," Knight countered and left the room before Day had a chance to respond.

Day ground his teeth for a few seconds. That guy was going to drive him insane. He wished he had someone else as his partner for his first assignment. Day closed the transmission files he'd been working on and saved them onto a USB stick so he could take them home. A grin formed on his face as he opened a window into the Scorpion internal systems and went to work, searching for information on Knighton. If he was going to be working with the man, he was going to find out everything there was to know about him. Fuck if he'd stumble around like some newbie and let Knight get the better of him all the time.

DIRK GREYSON is very much an outside kind of man. He loves travel and seeing new things. Dirk worked in corporate America for way too long and now spends his days writing, gardening, and taking care of the home he shares with his partner of more than two decades. He has a master's degree and all the other accessories that go with a corporate job. But he is most proud of the stories he tells and the life he's built. Dirk lives in Pennsylvania in a century-old home and is blessed with an amazing circle of friends.

Facebook: www.facebook.com/dirkgreyson
E-mail: dirkgreyson@comcast.net

DIRK GREYSON

SUN AND SHADOW

Day and Knight: Book 2
Sequel to *Day and Knight*

Dayton "Day" Ingram is recovering from an injury suffered in Mexico—and from his failed relationship with fellow Scorpion agent, Knight. While researching an old government document, Day realizes he might be holding the key to finding an artistic masterpiece lost since WWII.

But the Russians are looking for it too, and have a team in place in Eastern Europe hunting it down. Day and Knight are brought back together when they are charged with getting to the painting first.

Knight wants to leave Mexico and everything that happened there behind, and return to the life he had—except it wasn't much of a life. When he's partnered up with Day, keeping his distance proves to be challenging. But Day is as stubborn as Knight and isn't willing to let him walk away.

Their assignment leads them through Germany and Austria with agents hot on their tail—agents willing to do whatever it takes to get to the masterpiece first. If Day and Knight can live long enough to find the painting, they might also discover something even more precious—each other.

www.dreamspinnerpress.com

YELLOWSTONE WOLVES

CHALLENGE
the DARKNESS

Dirk Greyson

Yellowstone Wolves: Book 1

When alpha shifter Mikael Volokov is called to witness a challenge, he learns the evil and power-hungry Anton Gregor will stop at nothing to attain victory. Knowing he will need alliances to keep his pack together, Mikael requests a congress with the nearby Evergreen pack and meets Denton Arguson, Evergreen alpha, to ask for his help. Fate has a strange twist for both of them, though, and Mikael and Denton soon realize they're destined mates.

Denton resists the pull between them—he has his own pack and his own responsibilities. But Mikael isn't willing to give up. The Mother has promised Mikael his mate, told him he must fight for him, and that only together can they defeat the coming darkness. When Anton casts his sights on Denton's pack, attacks and sabotage follow, pulling Denton and Mikael together to defeat a common enemy. But Anton's threats sow seeds of destruction enough to break any bond, and the mates' determination to challenge the darkness may be their only saving grace.

www.dreamspinnerpress.com

YELLOWSTONE WOLVES

DARKNESS THREATENING

Dirk Greyson

Yellowstone Wolves: Book 2
Sequel to *Challenge the Darkness*

Fredrik is back from college and trying to stay out of his power-hungry brother's way, until his brother takes a prisoner for his pleasure. Unable to tolerate his family's cruelty, Fredrik overcomes his fear to help her escape back to her pack. There, he meets Christopher, and their instant attraction tells him Christopher is the one. However, since the threat of his brother remains, Fredrik is reluctant to pursue a relationship.

Christopher is still figuring out his place in the pack and has been living on his own to avoid making waves with his brother, Mikael. Now he's met his soulmate, and he'll do anything to take care of his love, including rejoining the pack.

With coaxing, Fredrik accepts his feelings, and Christopher's pack gives him the home he's never had. But Fredrick soon realizes he should keep running. His brother is on his tail and will stop at nothing to obtain the power he craves, especially when he realizes the source of the power could be Fredrik himself.

www.dreamspinnerpress.com

AN
ASSASSIN'S
HOLIDAY

DIRK
GREYSON

Brick Colton has been hired to kill Santa Claus—or at least the kindhearted accountant playing Santa for the kids in an orphanage. Brick grew up in an orphanage himself, but that isn't the only thing bothering him about the contract on Robin Marvington's life. The details don't add up, and it's looking more and more like someone has set Robin up. As Brick investigates, Robin brings some much-needed cheer into his life, the light in Robin's soul reaching something in Brick's dark one. But all of that will end if they can't find the person who wants Robin dead.